THE COTTAGE IN THE BOG

D0574079

The COTTAGE in the BOG

BY MAURA LAVERTY

with illustrations by
BARRY CASTLE

WITHDRAWN FROM STOCK

LIMERICK CITY LIBRARY

33892

Revised edition

TOWN
HOUSE

First published in 1945 by
Browne and Nolan Limited

This edition published in 1992 by
Town House
42 Morehampton Road
Donnybrook
Dublin 4

Copyright © Original text, Maura Laverty
Revised edition, Town House and Barry Castle, 1992
Illustrations, Barry Castle, 1992

British Library Cataloguing in Publication Data available

ISBN: 0-948524-44-8

Illustrations: Barry Castle
Design: Bill Murphy FCSD
Printed in Ireland by Criterion Press Ltd

My mother, Maura Laverty, was born in Rathangan, County Kildare, in 1907. Her father, Michael Kelly, a gambler first and farmer second, was from Kilkenny, as was her mother, Mary Anne, a dressmaker who had an establishment in Kilkenny town and was severe with her apprentices — and not interested in grandchildren.

My mother attended the Brigidine Convent in Tullow and from there, at the age of seventeen, she went to Spain as a governess. She taught herself some shorthand and became secretary to Prince Bibesco, a diplomat and husband of Princess Bibesco the writer. Later she worked for a bank and wrote for the Madrid newspaper El Debate. She was engaged to a Hungarian engineer who was working in Madrid and on her visit home before her wedding she met and married my father, James Laverty, a journalist with whom she had corresponded when in Spain. She went back to Madrid to explain to her Hungarian fiancé that she would not marry him, then returned to Dublin where she lived for the rest of her life.

She had three children, my sister, my brother and myself. She continued working as a journalist in Dublin and as a writer for radio programmes. Her first novel Never No More, written in 1942, was a big success. Three more novels followed, all of them successful, and then two children's books, cookery books and short stories. Two plays were very big hits, both in the same year. The second play, Tolka Row, became the first Irish TV drama series and ran for many years, continuing even after my mother's death in 1966.

I was born in Dublin and attended seven different schools. I went to the National College of Art but did not finish my studies because they thought I was wasting my time. I married the artist Phillip Castle in 1973 and now we both work as artists and live in France. I have illustrated two other books, Cooking for Cats (1988) and Cry Wolf (1988), both published by Methuen, London.

Barry Castle
March 1992

CHAPTER ONE

WHEN Essie reached the bend in the road she stood to wait for her brother. From where she stood she could see their cottage with its golden thatch of new straw shining brightly in the sun. The walls, which her father whitewashed every spring, were snowy as may-blossom. It was a long, low cottage with four rooms. Essie's mother and father slept in the end room. In the next room, which was the parlour, or "the best room" — as the Byrnes always called it — Essie slept in a special bed that every morning became a chair. Her father was a carpenter, and the chair-bed, which he made himself, had been his present for her twelfth birthday last November. The kitchen came next. This sometimes became a bedroom too, for Uncle Pat. He was the skipper of a canal boat, and when he stayed the night with them he slept in the settle-bed which stood beside the kitchen fire. The last room was shared by Granda and Essie's brother, Con. Granda was the oldest man in Glanaree and knew more about the ways of birds and animals than anyone living. At the rear-end of the house there was a built-on addition with a galvanised roof which her father, Jem, used as a workshop. The small garden in front of the cottage was bright with dog-daisies and red and yellow roses and tall purple lupins, and on the far side of the cottage, a rushy field stretched to the bog. Between the field and the sea of purple heather a hedge of rowans rose like a breakwater. Here the Byrnes' livestock grazed together in friendship — Betsy, the cow, and Shevawn, the goat, and Neddeen, the little black ass.

Essie noticed that Betsy was not in the field. She wondered if the cow had strayed and if she and her brother would have to go looking for her when they had eaten their dinner.

Essie waved to her mother at the cottage door. "Hurry up, Con," she called. "Mother is waiting for us." At first Con did not answer because he was wrestling with his friend, Mike Fahy. The three children always came home from school together. Mike was an orphan and lived with Big Bill in his tiny house about a half-mile beyond the Byrnes' cottage.

Neither Essie nor Con could remember Mike's parents, nor could Mike remember them himself. Big Bill had been their friend. When they had died and when no relatives had come forward to claim Mike, the kind-hearted peddler, who was once a sailor, had adopted the boy himself.

"Hurry, Con," Essie called again. "Our dinner will be cold." The mention of food could always make Con hurry when nothing else could. He broke away from Mike and the two boys came running up the road, their bare brown feet raising little clouds of white dust as they ran.

No three friends ever differed so much in looks as Essie and Con and Mike. Essie was like her mother, thin and small-boned, but she had her father's fairness, and her two long plaits were as yellow as butter. Con had his mother's colouring — dark grey eyes and curly, black hair. He was big for thirteen, and was already head and shoulders over Essie. He could run like the wind and for two years in succession he had won the prize for the junior race at Glanaree sports. Mike

8

was a stocky, thick-set lad, snub-nosed and freckled, with great strength in his arms. He was expected to win a place for himself in the county tug-of-war team.

The children were as different in character as in looks. Essie was quiet and gentle. Mike, though he was as fond of games as the next, liked to read best of all. Con was the wild one who didn't care if he never saw a book, and who was the ringleader in every adventure.

When the children reached the little bridge which spanned the brown stream that ran between the road and their gate, Bruss, the Irish terrier, roused himself from his sleep in the sun to bark a welcome to them. Mrs Byrne came to meet them. "Big Bill left word that he won't be back till late, Mike," she said. "You're to have your dinner with us. And he said you were to feed the hens and the pig and to milk the goat. He said he mightn't be able to get back at all tonight. If he doesn't, you can sleep with Con."

The two boys gave a whoop of delight. They always enjoyed the evenings they spent together when Big Bill's travels kept him from home. Mike loved to spend the night with the Byrnes, although he often thought he would enjoy himself more if Mrs Byrne had not such a love of soap and water. Big Bill was content if he merely washed his feet before going to bed, but Mrs Byrne was more particular. Still, he would have endured more than this for the pleasures that such evenings always brought.

Their dinner was waiting for them on the table, sending up clouds of steam and an appetising odour.

Con sniffed delightedly. "Pork stew!" he said with relish.

"Glutton!" his mother teased him. "Do you never think of anything but food and play?"

10

Mike looked up from his plate of stew. "We nearly forgot to tell you the good news, Mrs Byrne," he said. "We got our holidays today."

"So early?" Mrs Byrne marvelled, drawing a chair close to the window and settling herself to knit while the children ate. "June isn't finished yet, you never got them this early before."

"I know, mother," Con put in. "But the Carrolls have the measles and so have the Loughlins, so Dr Maher came in today and said the school was to be closed. Isn't it great? We'll have ten weeks' holidays."

"Great for you, son, but not for poor Mrs Carroll and Mrs Loughlin." Mrs Byrne cleared away the plates which the children had scraped clean. For dessert she gave each of them a blue-banded mug filled with creamy milk and a slice of fresh griddle-bread spread with jam. "What other news have you for me?" she asked.

"Mike won money in school," Essie told her. "The boys were told to write a composition about the bog, and Mike made up a poem. Mr Lawler said it showed great promise, and he gave Mike a prize."

"Well done," Mrs Byrne said with admiration. "Good boy, Mike. There's no one to beat you at putting words together." Mike blushed at the praise until his face was as red as his hair. Although there was nothing of the dreamy-eyed poet about Mike, whenever he took a pencil in his hand the words seemed to flow out of it. Mr Lawler often read out his compositions for the whole school.

"Read the poem for me, Mike," Mrs Byrne said.

"Go on, Mike," Con encouraged. "You have it there in your copybook."

"Wait a minute," Mrs Byrne told them. "We'll get Granda

in to hear it too. He's out in the byre." She went to the door and called. The old man came, leaning heavily on his stick. Granda was crippled with rheumatism, but he said his blackthorn stick was as good to him as a pair of new legs. Laughter seemed to lurk in every wrinkle of his face — or, it should be said, in as much of his face as was not hidden by his bushy white beard and whiskers. He was every bit as fond of fun as the children. If there was any mischief afoot, he was sure to have a part in it, and when the children got into trouble he could always be counted on to do his best for them. "Let them off just this once," he would plead.

"Good boy Mike!" he cried, when he heard the news. "Big Bill will be proud when he hears this! Read out the poem, son."

"I'd rather Essie read it," Mike said shyly. So Essie read it while Mike did his best to look unconcerned.

> Down in the bog when day awakes
> The sun bends down and gently takes
> The veil of mist from the purple land,
> And birdsong rises on every hand.
>
> Down in the bog in noon-day's heat
> The workmen save the good brown peat.
> Among the heather the rabbits play,
> And willows dance in the breezes gay.
>
> Down in the bog at evening's fall
> The dusk is filled with the curlews' call
> Till night creeps up on quiet feet
> To wrap the heather and birds and peat.

When Mrs Byrne and Granda had finished praising Mike's poem, Essie took the tin basin from under the kitchen table. She filled it with water from the kettle that hung on a crane over the fire and she and Con started to do the washing-up. Mike took a bucket and set off for the well at the bottom of the field.

"Did you tell Essie about the cow?" Granda asked Mrs Byrne.

Essie turned quickly. "What is it, Granda?"

"You'd never guess, Essie," her mother said. "Betsy calved today."

Essie put down the plate she was drying. Her face grew pink with excitement and her blue eyes danced. "Oh, mother! And you waited all this time to tell me! Where is the calf? How is it? What is it like?"

"Take your time, love," laughed Mrs Byrne. "I didn't tell you when you came in, because I knew if I did you wouldn't eat a bite of your dinner. You would have been outside with the calf, hugging it and talking to it."

Essie loved everything that was small and young and weak. In springtime, she was often late for school. She could never bear to pass a field where there were young lambs. She would climb through the hedge and sit fondling the warm-coated little creatures. Father Brophy had come upon her one morning as he walked along the road. Essie was kneeling in Flynn's field with two new-born lambs, an arm holding each of them close. When she glanced up and saw the priest looking at her over the hedge, she hung her head and waited for the scolding she knew she deserved for being late for school. But Father Brophy had only said gently, "Isn't it time you were at your lessons?"

13

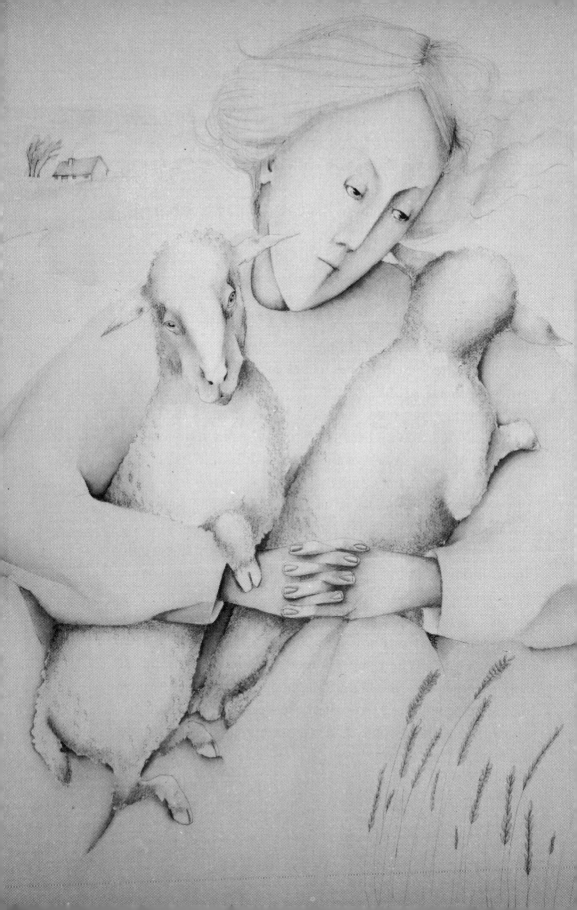

She was all eagerness to see the new calf. She ran out to the byre at the back of the house, and she gave a soft cry of delight when her eyes fell on Betsy's baby. There it stood, beautifully marked with brown and white patches. Essie walked towards it very quietly so as not to frighten it, but the calf was not afraid. It seemed to know that Essie had nothing but love for it. On thin unsteady legs the calf went to meet her. Her heart beat wildly as her arms went about it, and she rubbed her warm cheek against its muzzle, black and cool and moist. The she heard her mother's voice. "Come in and finish the washing-up, Essie," Mrs Byrne called. "The calf won't run away, never you fear."

Mike came in with the brimming bucket of water and set it carefully on the wooden bench, where it was always kept so as to be well out of reach of the inquisitive beaks of the hens that darted into the kitchen whenever the half-door was left open.

As soon as the children had finished their jobs, they asked Mrs Byrne if they could go and gather strawberries. She agreed, but added in a strict voice, "Don't be late home. Your father likes you to be here when he comes in to his supper, and don't forget, Mike, that you have to be back to milk Big Bill's goat and feed the pig and hens. You'd better start for home as soon as you hear the evening church bell."

"We won't forget," the children promised. "We'll be home early."

Essie hugged her mother, and the boys hurried to take down from the dresser the three tin mugs they hoped to fill with strawberries.

CHAPTER TWO

MIKE and Essie turned towards the grove, but Con stopped them.

"There's not much use in looking for strawberries in the grove," he said. "We picked cans of them there last week."

"That's right," Mike agreed. "And the gang of lads that came out from the town last Sunday got what was left. The grove's picked clean."

"Where will we try, then?" Essie asked. "Will we go to the Black Bog?"

"No — it's too far," Con said. "I know a nearer place. It's better too."

"Where, Con?"

Con lowered his voice. "The rath behind the Big House."

"Oh, Con!" Essie's eyes grew round. "You wouldn't dare!"

"Don't be daft, Con," Mike said. "You know that McFadden goes raging mad if anyone puts a foot near his place. He might set that big brute of a dog on us. Surely you wouldn't go there after the way he chased Shamie Dunne with a stick last summer?"

"Why not?" Con retorted. "Everybody knows that rath is the best place in Glanaree for strawberries. It's where Granda used to gather them when he was a boy. Mother used to gather them there too. You heard her yourself saying that it

was always red with strawberries — great big juicy ones."
"Yes Con," Mike agreed, beginning to weaken.

"I think it's a shame," Con went on, "that the strawberries are let rot there year after year just because people are too much afraid of old McFadden to go and pick them. Well, I'm not afraid of him. I'm going to pick a mugful there this evening. You two needn't come if you're frightened."

"I'm not frightened," Mike said quickly. "If you're going, I'll go with you. What about you, Essie?"

"If the two of you are going, so am I," Essie said excitedly. "I only hope old McFadden doesn't catch us, that's all."

"We won't make any noise," Con planned. "He'll never know we're there. And even if he catches us, he can't kill us for gathering a few strawberries that would only go to waste if we didn't pick them."

"And anyway, we can run faster than he can," Mike argued.

"We wouldn't be able to run faster than the dog, though," Essie pointed out a little fearfully.

"You needn't be afraid of the dog, Essie," Mike said kindly. "The old dog is always at the front of the house — we'll be around at the back. Come on. It'll be a bit of fun, anyway."

"I suppose it will," Essie agreed. She began to look forward to the adventure. A thought struck her. "Couldn't we take Neddeen?" she suggested. "It's a good bit to McFadden's place. We could take turns riding. And if he does chase us, Neddeen will help us to get away quicker."

The boys thought this a good idea and Con ran back to the house for the reins while Mike caught the little ass and led him on to the road. Essie had the first ride, and her lively donkey trotted nimbly up the road, his dainty black hooves striking a muffled note through the layers of dust. Mike ran by Neddeen's head, while Con followed eagerly.

Mr McFadden, the owner of Glanaree House, or the Big House, as the children always called it, was a silent, forbidding man who was feared by every child in the area. Grown-ups feared him too, as much for his evil looks as for the mystery with which he had surrounded himself. Twenty years before, the people of Glanaree had been thrilled to hear that the Big House, which had stood empty for so long, had been bought by a rich man, and that the new owner was coming to live among them. It pleased them to think that now there would be life and gaiety in the old place, and constant work for the locals, while the local gentry smiled at the thought of the grand balls and parties in store for them.

But they were all mistaken. The new owner proved to be a gaunt, sandy-haired man with foxy eyes and with furtive craftiness written in every line of him. He brought with him a man-servant who was as unlikeable looking as his master. The men and women who presented themselves at the back door in the hope of getting work were told rudely to take themselves off, with the threat that if they came again the dog would be set on them. To the visitors who called in the hope of making friends, McFadden made it plain that he wanted none of them, and the shopkeepers who came looking for his custom were told that he had made arrangements to have all his supplies sent from Clonboyle, a neighbouring town. All in all, McFadden let it be seen that he intended to have nothing to do with the people of Glanaree. He went further. He showed that he would stop at nothing to keep them out. Not even the postman was to be allowed near the house. A locked

19

letter-box was fixed to the front gate, at which a huge Alsatian kept constant guard, and McFadden doubled the height of the stone wall that enclosed the house, shrubberies, orchard and the ruined castle to the left of the house in which, it was said, kings had lived in days gone by — those kings who had given Glanaree, or the Glen of the Kings, its name.

The people of Glanaree were proud and they did not force themselves on the harsh hermit. As the years went by he became more and more morose, until those who might meet him during his solitary walks through the bog at night did not dare to salute him. They knew their greeting would be ignored or answered with a snarl. So they left him to himself, and gradually they even gave up guessing at what had brought him here, or what grim secrets the old house might hold.

In spite of the June sun, which shone so warmly on heather and gorse and delicate wild rose, the children shivered when they came within sight of Glanaree House. That gloomy grey wall gave it the look of a prison, and a chilling air of silence hung over it.

"I hope the old dog doesn't start barking," Con said.

"I think we're safe enough from him," Mike said. He was right. The house was built with its side to the road. The dog was always just inside the front gate, and since the wind was blowing from the Black Bog it swept past the dog, carrying the children's scent away from him.

With rising excitement, they continued along the road until they came to where the side wall of the orchard ended and a wooden gate marked the beginning of a lane in which docks and thistle had long blotted out the tracks of human feet. The lane ran along the back of the orchard right up to the rath

20

LIMERICK COUNTY LIBRARY
33892

where the strawberries grew. They tethered Neddeen to the gate-post. He sank his muzzle into the cool green sweetness of the lush grass and started to munch.

The children climbed over the gate with careful quietness, and started up the lane. "Go easy," Essie whispered. "Don't make a sound." Mike and Con did not heed her warning, and when they came to a small wooden door in the wall they hardly dared to breathe for fear that McFadden himself might be lurking on the other side. Twice during that breathless tip-toeing walk from gate to rath, Essie felt a strong inclination to make a bolt for the road and safety — once, when a stony-hammer with a violent whirr of wings darted out from a hole in the wall right into her face, and again, when a plover rose with a squawk of surprise from the tangle beneath their feet and fluttered lop-sidedly out over the bog.

At last they reached the end of the lane. In front of them was the rath, a mossy mound crowned with a half-dozen gnarled and stunted trees. Their mother had not exaggerated. It was red with strawberries — bigger and redder wild strawberries than the children had ever seen. Heavy-headed, the strawberries drooped on their stems, as if they had given up hope of being gathered.

"Now, aren't you glad we came here?" Con exulted.

Mike answered him by eagerly bending to pick. In the pleasure of gathering the abundant ripe fruit, their fears left them. Plainly, they had not disturbed the occupants of Glanaree House, and the only disquieting sound to be heard was a kind of infrequent scraping which seemed to come from inside the rath.

"What would that be?" Essie asked. "Listen..."

The boys listened. "Only a rabbit burrowing," Con assured

22

her. "Let's hurry up and get the mugs filled."

Mike's face was troubled. It *might* be a rabbit, but rabbits burrowed with their claws and the sound their burrowing made was dull and muffled. Mike thought that in the scraping that came to them now and then from beneath their feet there was the distinct clink of metal on stone. But since the others did not appear to have noticed this, he decided that he was imagining things, and he continued to pick.

Though they ate as they picked, it did not take long to fill the mugs, and then the children took long wiry stalks of wild wheat and threaded the berries onto them. The tassel at the end of each stalk made a stopper which prevented the fruit from sliding off. It seemed to them that they had only begun to pick when the church bell rang out, sending its mellow chime over the bog.

"Come on," Mike said. "We promised your mother we'd leave for home as soon as the bell went. Don't forget that I've to feed the hens and milk the goat on the way home."

"I suppose we'd better go," Con said regretfully. "But I hate leaving all these strawberries behind us."

"Can't we come again tomorrow?" Essie suggested. "Nothing happened to us today, and we know now we needn't be so scared any more."

As they walked down the lane under the high orchard wall the bog lay stretched before them in waves of blue and purple, with the heaps of brown turf looking like sturdy brown boats. On every turf-bank they could see the workers preparing for home. These familiar sights had a reassuring effect on the children, making them overlook the fact that they were not yet out of the danger zone, and they laughed and shouted merrily as they hurried to where Neddeen waited. It was only as they passed the low wooden door that they suddenly remembered the need for caution, but then it was too late. Their hearts stood still as they heard behind them the grating of a rusty key in a lock and the creaking of disused hinges.

"Come spying on me, would you?" a harsh voice shouted. "I'll teach you!"

Petrified, the children stood and looked back. The owner of Glanaree House was struggling through the half-open door. His pale face was twisted with rage, and a red light of fury flamed in his eyes.

"Come back here," he snarled, brandishing a heavy stick. "Come back till I show you how I deal with spies!"

"Run for it lads!" Con shouted.

Terror lent them speed and like three frightened hares they raced for the gate while McFadden loped in their wake, shouting for his dog as he ran. But the three chums had had a good start, and they were out on the road with Neddeen untethered while their pursuer was still twenty yards from the gate, and while the dog's answer was still only an angry bark in the distance.

Essie clambered onto Neddeen's back, Con gave the little ass a hard slap on the rump, and the four of them were off — galloping ass, racing boys and bobbing, jolting Essie, leaving McFadden to shout his threats into the cloud of dust raised by their heels.

Not until they were half-way home did they ease up. To their dismay, they found they had lost most of their strawberries.

"To think we had all that fright for nothing," Essie said as she realised her mug was missing.

24

They looked at each other dolefully until Con said: "Well, we gave old McFadden a run for his money!"

This was certainly true, and now that the danger was safely past it was easy to think of that fearful rush down the lane as a great bit of fun. By the time they reached Big Bill's house, they were even able to laugh about it. At the same time, they realised that it would have been no laughing matter had McFadden caught them, or if his dog had been with him in the orchard. Essie voiced the general feeling when she said that not for all the strawberries in Ireland would she face up that lane again. They sent the ass home before them and pushed open the five-barred gate leading into Big Bill's yard. The hens ran clucking to them and the pig snorted a noisy welcome from his sty.

"We'll all give a hand, Mike," Con offered. "I'll milk the goat and Essie can feed the hens while you feed the pig. We'll be finished in no time."

Big Bill's two-roomed cabin stood on a little patch of ground that had been reclaimed from the bog. The house and the land attached to it were small but, as Big Bill said, they held everything any reasonable man and boy could ask of life. There was a strip of grazing for the jennet, and for the shaggy-bearded grey goat that gave them milk. There was a nice little piece of garden for potatoes and cabbage and onions. A good share of the potatoes went to the hens and to the fat pink pig which would give them bacon to eat with their cabbage and rasher gravy for their bread. Unlike many of the other people around, who raised pigs for sale, Big Bill kept his pigs for food. When he needed money to buy clothes for Mike and himself or to pay the rent, he yoked the jennet and set out over the countryside to peddle his wares. In the back of his cart were baskets filled with buttons and combs and cheery delf, and such things as needles and thread. The people who lived far from town and shops were glad to buy from him and he always returned from his trips with the money he needed.

Taking the key from its hiding-place in the cranny beside the door-post, Mike opened the door. It was a snug place with its clean-swept earthen floor and its dresser of bright dishes. From the top of the dresser two white china spaniels with brown ears looked down at the red curtains and the oilcloth-covered table and the shelves which held Mike's books — all of them presents from Big Bill, who rarely returned from a trip without a book for Mike. A door at the right of the fireplace led into the bedroom. Con had a great envy of his friend's sleeping-quarters, for it wasn't on ordinary beds that Mike and Big Bill slept, but in real sailor's bunks built one over the other.

Con took a tin can and went out to milk the goat, while Mike and Essie started to prepare the food. Before leaving, Big Bill had hung a pot of potatoes on the crane over the fire. For hours they had simmered gently on the greying turf, and now they were cooked to mushiness — just the way the pig and hens liked them. Essie helped Mike to lift the pot off the crane. Between them they carried it to the door. Mike held a piece of sack over the pot while he tilted it sideways to strain off the water. Some of the potatoes were put into a tin basin for the hens and a few handfuls of bran mixed in as well.

"Here, chuck-chuck-chuck!" Essie called, carrying the basin out to the yard. Eager clucking started as the hens came hurtling from all directions towards their supper, necks craning stiffly and scaly feet scattering gravel and dust. She

27

put the basin on the ground and they threw themselves on it, shouldering and jostling each other so as to perch on its rim. She left them to their meal and went back to Mike, who was pouring buttermilk into the bucket of potatoes and meal he had mixed for the pig. The pig had smelt the food. He was snorting with impatience and trying to poke his snout through the six-inch space between the bottom of the sty door and the ground. Essie held the door open while Mike carried in the bucket of mash and emptied it into the trough. With little grunts of happiness, the pig gobbled.

By now, the hens had eaten their supper though they still pecked at the basin so as not to lose even the smallest scrap of food.

"Into your beds," Mike teased them as he shooed them into their house where they fluttered on to the roost, and started to settle themselves comfortably for the night. A few of the more particular ones did a hurried toilet, combing out their breast feathers with their beaks, and poking beneath their wings for stray insects. But the majority didn't bother with such preparations, they simply hunched themselves so as to bring up their shoulder feathers, and let their heads sink into them. They blinked their beady eyes at Mike and Essie who were collecting the eggs from the row of hay-filled nests opposite the perch.

Con whistled. "Here's the milk," he called. "She gave a great canful this evening."

When the eggs were put on the dresser, the milk strained into a bowl, and the can and strainer washed, they were free to lock the door and run down the road towards their own supper.

When they came in sight of the cottage, they saw a man

cycling from the opposite direction. He got off his bike at the cottage gate and waved to them. "It's Uncle Pat!" shouted Essie in delight.

"Uncle Pat!" shouted Con and Mike together. They raced towards him. The little wiry man in the navy serge suit who was skipper of the *Maggie May* was a great favourite with the three children. And with good reason. He gave them lots of trips up the canal on his boat.

"Are you staying the night, Uncle Pat?" Essie asked, hanging out of one of his arms and Mike out of the other, while Con wheeled in the bike.

"I will if your mother doesn't throw me out," Uncle Pat said, his eyes twinkling in his brown face in the very same way as Granda's. This was great news, because when Uncle Pat slept in the house they were always let stay up late.

Mrs Byrne sat at the top of the full table later on. Her husband sat at the other end of the table, a placid, easy-going man with a round, pleasant face and fair hair that was going thin on top. Jem Byrne never had much to say. Granda said that was because the rest of the family did his share of the talking as well as their own. But Jem liked hearing the others talk. The three children sat together at one side. They were hurrying through their supper so as to start on the yard-long ribbons of liquorice which Uncle Pat had brought them. With the excitement of Uncle Pat's arrival, Mrs Byrne had forgotten about the strawberries, and so they were pleased not to have to make excuses for coming home empty-handed.

Half-way through supper, Uncle Pat clapped his hand to his forehead. "Well, I have a head like a sieve. Imagine me forgetting to give you Aunt Sarah's letter." Mrs Byrne took the letter and started to read it.

30

"Why doesn't Aunt Sarah ever come down to see us?" Essie asked, remembering suddenly that they had only been brought to Dublin once to see her, when they were very small.

"She says she's too old," Granda said. "That the journey down here would be the death of a woman of her age." Granda snorted indignantly. "Old! The woman is only — let me see — three years younger than myself, and I'm only seventy-six. Old, how are you? Sure, she's only a girl. I think that city life must make people old before their time."

"I'd like to see her," Con said. "She was nice to us that time we went to Dublin. I don't remember her very well, but I remember she gave me a big box of sweets."

Mrs Byrne looked up from her letter. "You might be seeing her soon. She says here I'm to send you up for a couple of days. Yourself and Essie, and Mike too, if Big Bill will let him — she says the three of you will be welcome."

The children looked at each other, speechless with delight.

"Well, doesn't that sound great!" Mr Byrne said, well pleased at the treat in store for them.

"It'd be nice for them, Jem," Mrs Byrne said slowly, "but the question is: Who's going to take them up to Dublin and bring them home again? I wouldn't like to trust three wild things like these on a bus by themselves. I can't go, and you can't go with them. They'd never be safe on their own."

The children were starting to protest when Uncle Pat put in a word. "Would you trust them to me, Mary?" he asked. "I'm taking the *Maggie May* up to Dublin on Monday. I want to get her engine overhauled, so I'll be staying in Dublin for three or four days. They could go up with me and come back with me, and I'll guarantee they'll be as right as rain."

Mrs Byrne looked at her husband. "That sounds a good plan, Jem. What do you think?"

"The best ever," he agreed. "A great plan."

Essie, Con and Mike agreed with him fully. To spend a few days in Dublin would be great, but to go and return on the *Maggie May* would be heaven itself.

That night they could talk of nothing but Dublin and excited plans for the trip. When at last they said a sleepy good-night, Mike put the feelings of the three of them in a nutshell. "The holidays have really got off to a great start," he said.

CHAPTER THREE

THE sky was flushed when they awakened next day. By mid-morning, it had turned to silver-grey and by the time the three children were returning from Big Bill's place where they had done an equal share of the tasks, a fine misty rain was falling. They ran for the shelter of the cottage.

Granda was leaning on the half-door, looking out into a world that was full of sweet scents released by the rain. He opened the door and stood aside as they ran in past him, their hair beaded with raindrops and their faces glistening.

Mrs Byrne looked up from the nettles she was chopping for the hens. "Dry your heads immediately," she told them. "If I hear a cough or a sniffle, there will be no trip to Dublin next week." This threat made Con and Mike rub until their heads were like hedgehogs.

"If you'd only use your eyes, you'd never get caught out in the rain," Granda said, limping to his chair by the fire. "We've been having signs of it all the week — the frogs turning dark brown and the spiders spinning thick webs and the sheep huddling together under the trees, and the cat cleaning her whiskers till she has them nearly rubbed off."

Con wanted to change the subject.

"Could we do anything to help you, mother?" he asked.

"I don't think there's anything, son," she said. "There's

plenty of turf in, and water, and your Granda washed the potatoes for me. I think the best way the three of you could help me would be to take yourselves from under my feet. Go into the workshop and play there till the rain's over. If I want you for anything, I'll call you."

"I'll go with you." Granda rose stiffly and followed them. "I've wax melted to make a few candles — Essie can help me. And I cut a couple of grand willow sticks this morning. Maybe Con and Mike would like to make a whistle or two out of them."

The boys were delighted with the suggestion. They liked using their hands. Ever since they had been big enough to be allowed the use of tools, they had made their own playthings. They had lovely big kites that could soar as high as an aeroplane, and which they made by pasting sheets of paper over light pieces of wood and string. From the quiet canal they brought home many a fish caught with their home-made rods — long, straight joints of hazel, with floats that were just big corks bored through with a red-hot knitting-needle. They made suckers too, which gave them plenty of sport in weight-lifting contests. The suckers were round pieces of leather cut from the tops of old boots, and then soaked in water and hammered until they were soft. A hole was punched in the centre and a string with a knot on the end drawn through. When a sucker was wet and pressed onto a flat stone with your foot, you could lift the stone even if it weighed as much as yourself.

Essie knew how to make her toys too. There were twenty things at her hand from which she could make little dolls. She had made a whole family of dolls from the tufts of wool which the sheep left on the thorny bushes as they went

34

through a gap. First, the tuft was teased out until it was fine and silky. A long thick strand, doubled, made head, body and legs. Half an inch from the top, a scrap of cotton was wound around the strand. When the wool above this tie was clipped, you had the doll's fuzzy hair. An inch down, another tie was made, and here, when eyes and nose and mouth were embroidered on with coloured threads, you had the doll's little face. Four inches further down, a third tie was made to form the doll's body. The rest of the strand was divided in two for the legs, and a tie made at each ankle. Now a second strand, shorter and thinner than the first, was pushed through the body to form the arms, and when the doll's wrists had been formed with a twist of thread, the little cuddly thing was ready to be dressed. Dolls could be made from potatoes, too, funny brown-faced dolls, that stood dumpily on four bits of stick.

But the dolls Essie liked best, and the most easily made, were the dainty little dancing dolls which she made with the wild poppies that flamed among the long grasses. You had to be careful to choose a poppy with a good thick stem, a stem thick enough to split with your nail into two legs for the doll. Very, very gently, so as not to break them off, you turned the delicate petals down over the little legs, and then you tied them in place at the waist with a blade of grass, leaving the two ends of the blade standing out to make the dancer's arms. You didn't have to do another thing, her beautiful skirts of silky red stood out about her, her wild gypsy hair the tufted black centre of the poppy.

Bruss, the dog, followed the four of them into the workshop.

They set to work, Granda and Essie on their candle-making, Con and Mike on the willow sticks.

Con was soon lost in his job, and he whistled happily as he cut and whittled, in his favourite place. He loved everything in the workshop, the clean smell of the wood, the tidy rows of sharp bright tools, the sturdy bench and the tin boxes of gleaming nails. He was looking forward to the day when he would leave school and join his father here.

Mike was restless. He kept going to the window and looking up the rain-washed road.

"What is wrong with you, Mike?" Granda asked. "You're as fidgety as a hen on a hot griddle."

"I wish Big Bill was back," Mike said.

"He will soon be home, never fear," Granda assured him. "A man who sailed the seven seas in his time will come home all right from a little journey of twenty or thirty miles." Granda began to prepare the mould in which he made the candles. Since the war, candles were a scarce commodity around Glanaree, so whenever he had some beeswax, Granda made one or two. The mould was the outer case of an old bicycle pump. First, the wick had to be prepared. For this he used a length of thick white cotton from the remains of an old knitted quilt which Mrs Byrne had given him for the purpose. "Unravel a bit of that for me, Essie," Granda said. "Your eyes are better than mine."

Essie started to unravel the cotton. As he waited, Granda said, suddenly, "I've a crow to pluck with you, miss."

Essie looked up. "What is it, Granda? What did I do?"

The old man made his voice sound huffy. "There was I the whole of yesterday evening thinking of the lovely saucer of strawberries I would have for my tea and you never brought me home as much as one."

36

Essie reddened with guilt and the children looked at each other. They had decided not to tell of their adventure with McFadden for fear they would be scolded for going into danger. But Granda was different. They told him the whole story.

"You won't tell on us, will you, Granda?" Con begged.

Granda was indignant. "Did I ever tell on you?" he demanded. "Answer me that."

"No, Granda," they assured him. "Never once."

"Well then, I'm not going to start now." But he looked at them gravely. "Just the same, I'd keep away from McFadden's place, if I was you. It's my belief the man's not right in his head — nor the fellow who works for him, either. That pair are neither good nor lucky, and you'd be as well not to cross them."

"You won't catch me going near them again," Essie said. "Here's the bit of cotton for you, Granda. Is it long enough?"

He measured it against the length of the mould. "Fine," he said, "Fine."

"It'd take more than strawberries to make me put a foot near McFadden's place," Con said. "Just the same, I'd give a lot to know what he's hiding up there. He *must* be hiding something or he wouldn't be so set on keeping everyone away. I wonder what it could be, Granda?"

"Heaven only knows, son," Granda told him. He was stopping up the end of the mould with a round of cardboard so that the melted beeswax would not run out. Now the wick had to be set in place. With his gnarled hands, he made a knot in the length of cotton Essie had unravelled for him and drew it through a little hole in the cardboard. He pulled the cotton up to the mouth of the mould and made it taut by tying it to a match laid across the mouth. As he worked, he talked. "There are many who would like to know what brought McFadden down here to bury himself in the heart of the bog where he was a stranger to all of us. We made all kinds of guesses when he came first. Some said the police were after him, but they must have been wrong or he'd be in jail by now. Others thought he was a writer, maybe, that came here to write his books in peace. That couldn't have been true either, because if he was a writer Father Brophy or the schoolmaster would surely have heard of him. And I said he might be a monk of some sort who was under a vow to live a kind of hermit's life and speak to no one. That guess was as far out as all the others, for, as you know yourselves, McFadden doesn't go to church, chapel or meeting-house. And, anyway, if he was a man of God, he wouldn't hate his fellows the way he does. If you love God, you'll love people."

"There wasn't much love in McFadden's face when he was shouting at us yesterday evening," Con laughed. He had his whistle made except for the finishing touches. He put it to his lips and tried it. It gave a clear sweet note.

"I think myself there's no mystery at all about the old rascal," Granda said. "Like many another in the place, I wasted plenty of time puzzling my head over him and now I've come to the conclusion that he's an unfortunate old miser who's not right in the head. And that's why I'm warning you to keep out of his way — I don't believe he's responsible for his actions."

Essie shivered, remembering again the fury in those foxy eyes. She needed no warning to keep away from Glanaree House. Mike said nothing. He was remembering something too — that curious scraping sound that had come from inside the rath. The more he thought about it, the more he doubted it had been made by a rabbit.

Granda handed Essie the prepared mould. "Here, love," he said. "Hold this steady for me while I pour in the wax." Essie held it as steady as a house while the old man trickled in the melted wax.

Soon Big Bill arrived.

"Is there anyone here belonging to me?"

The ex-sailor was so tall and broad that the workshop seemed crowded when he came in. His face was as brown as leather, and his keen grey eyes had a web of little wrinkles about them from being screwed up against sun and wind.

"What's this I hear about you wanting to go gallivanting off to Dublin next week?" he asked Mike. "I met Uncle Pat on the road and he told me all about it."

"Won't you let me go, Big Bill?" Mike begged.

"Sure I'll let you." Big Bill would not have denied any child a treat. "What's more, I'm going with you myself. When I met Uncle Pat he was in a terrible sweat in case he wouldn't be sailing after all, as he was just after getting word that Tommy Dunne, the cook, broke his arm in a fight. I offered to take on Tommy's work for the trip, so it's all settled. I'll be sleeping on the boat while we're in Dublin, but I'll call for the three of you every morning and take you out to see the sights."

This was great news! With Big Bill to take them around, their stay in Dublin would be twice as exciting.

"Well, what have the three of you been up to while I was away?" Big Bill asked.

"We got our holidays yesterday," Mike told him. "We've nearly ten weeks. When we get back from Dublin I'll help you to draw home the turf." His face was alight with pleasure now that his Big Bill was home. Although Granda and Jem and Mrs Byrne were kind to him, Mike was always lonely when Big Bill went on his trips.

"Ten weeks' holidays?" Big Bill echoed. "Poor Mr Moran will never tame you when he gets you back."

"McFadden chased us yesterday evening," Con said. "But we're keeping it a secret, so don't tell."

"Mike won a shilling for making up a poem," Essie said.

"I'm pleased with you, Mike." It was plain that Big Bill was delighted with the boy. "Keep it up, son. Who knows but that some day we might be able to give you the schooling you're always wishing for. I have a prize for you too — a great big book about the Holy Land. I swapped a brown teapot for it with a woman over in Brackna." His voice changed as he asked: "But what's this Con said about McFadden?"

The big man was angry when he heard the whole story.

"Well, isn't he the crabbed, cross-grained puckawn of a man! He deserves to be punished for frightening the children like that and they not doing a bit of harm in the wide world. I've a good mind to go up and give him something to be sorry for."

"Don't," Granda urged. "Leave him to God. The peaceful way is the best way. Take no heed of him."

"But he's a menace around the place! He shouldn't be let carry on the way he does — frightening children."

"If the children would keep away from him, they needn't have any fear," Granda said reasonably. "With all his faults, I never heard tell of McFadden turning on anyone that kept out of his path. And, anyway — who knows? — he might pack up one day and be off as sudden as he came."

"It doesn't look like it," Big Bill said. "When I was passing his place, I saw a lorry delivering big wooden boxes of stuff. A Dublin lorry it was. If it was food in the crates, I'd say McFadden intends to stay here another twenty years."

Mrs Byrne's voice called from the kitchen. "Your dinner is on the table. I put your name in the pot too, Mike, and Big Bill's as well. Come and take it now while it's hot."

They needed no urging. In dealing with the cabbage and bacon and floury new potatoes, McFadden was forgotten.

42

CHAPTER FOUR

W HEN Monday morning came, everyone in the cottage was up at cockcrow. Essie and Mike were dressed and ready long before breakfast was on the table. Their mother had a basket to pack for Aunt Sarah — eggs and butter and a big home-made cake. Jem Byrne had a present to pack for her too — a set of shining wooden egg-cups which he had made and polished himself.

Granda was missing. He had taken his stick and had gone out early, no one knew where.

"I wish he was back," Mrs Byrne said worriedly as she set the pan on the fire. "He's so bad on his legs that I'm always afraid of him falling into a bog-hole. If he isn't in by the time the kettle comes to the boil you ought to go out and look for him, Jem."

"I'll do that," he promised. There was no need for him to go after all. At the very moment that the spout of the kettle started to spit angrily into the ashes, Granda came in. He carried a bunch of white heather.

"Give this to your Aunt Sarah from me," he told Essie. "Tell her I gathered it in the fox-covert in the very place where herself and myself used to gather it sixty or seventy years ago."

"I'll tell her, Granda." Essie took the heather and arranged it prettily in a little rush basket.

Mrs Byrne put a dish of golden rashers on the table and started to pour the tea. The children were so excited that they didn't want to eat, but Mrs Byrne insisted. They had arranged to meet Uncle Pat at Shane lock, where the *Maggie May* was moored. Big Bill was to drive them the eleven miles to Shane. His jennet and cart would be left in the care of the lock-keeper until their return.

They had barely finished breakfast when the cart drew up at the gate. It was then the fuss and bustle began, with the children running here and there to say goodbye, Jem Byrne hurrying from house to cart with parcels, Granda shouting advice on how they were to protect their lives and their pockets in the Dublin streets, Mother giving last-minute messages for Aunt Sarah and dire warnings about good behaviour, and Bruss yapping with such excitement that you'd think it was he who was off for a holiday in the city. Finally, the last parcel was handed up, the last message given and the last goodbye said. Big Bill gave a jerk to the reins and they were off, Essie sitting beside Big Bill on the cross-board, Granda's basket of white heather on her lap, Mike and Con in the back of the cart, with their legs dangling out over the tail-board.

They left the jennet and cart with the lock-keeper. Carrying their parcels, they made their way to where the *Maggie May* was moored a little above the lock. She was loaded with a cargo of turf. Sitting on deck with his back resting comfortably against the turf was a scrawny little man. He was Dinny Smullen, the deck-hand. He had a battered old hat pulled down over his eyes to shade them from the sun and nothing could be seen of his face but his bristly beard which

44

jutted out at right angles to his chin. He was fast asleep. Near to him a little pink pig was tethered by the leg to a mooring ring.

Con and Mike looked at each other in dismay when they saw Dinny. In their excitement about the trip, they had forgotten the fact that Dinny was very bad friends with them. The last time they had been on the boat they had upset a pot of tar on the deck while wrestling. Dinny idolised the *Maggie May*. He was very proud of the neat way he kept the boat and he was so furious with the boys that he had sworn he was finished with them.

"Ahoy, there, Dinny!" Big Bill called. His shout, which would have travelled across the Gulf of Persia, not only wakened Dinny, but brought Uncle Pat hurrying on deck.

The skipper of the *Maggie May* had a great welcome for all of them. Dinny's welcome was not so general. For Big Bill he had a hearty handshake, and for Essie a wide grin, but for the two boys he had nothing but a stony stare.

Uncle Pat noticed Dinny's coolness. "You're not still thinking about the little drop of tar, man?" he asked.

"Little drop of tar?" he said angrily? "They spilt as much over my clean deck as would tar a battleship. I nearly wore my hands away to the wrists trying to get it off?"

He looked very angry as he stamped off to start the engine.

"Don't worry, lads," Uncle Pat said. "He'll get over it all right. I often saw him that way before, and it fizzled out."

"Indeed," Big Bill agreed. "Dinny's bark is worse than his bite. Well, I'm going below to see about starting the dinner. Do you want to stow away your parcels?"

The children followed Big Bill down the ladder into the neat little cabin. It held a stove and washbasin and press, and two bunks which, during the day, served as seats. The table was a flap of wood which could be fastened back to the wall when not wanted. The walls were papered with the Christmas calendars which for thirty years Dinny had been collecting from every shopkeeper between Shane and Dublin.

Big Bill had brought four tender rabbits to make a stew for the dinner.

"Couldn't we help?" Mike asked. "Peel potatoes or something?"

"You could," Big Bill said gratefully, and in five minutes they were sitting cross-legged on deck with a bucket of potatoes and another bucket containing clean water into which they dropped the potatoes as they peeled.

"Who owns the little pig, Dinny?" Essie asked.

"It's for a woman who lives in Athy," Dinny answered.

"I paid a lot of money for it at the fair in Shane yesterday. I will be in trouble if anything happens to it."

They floated smoothly between the green banks, on each side of which the rushy land sloped quickly into fertile fields. In some of these the brown and white cattle were growing big and fat on juicy grass and contentment. In others, the young wheat was a greeny-yellow sea, across which a deeper wave of colour sometimes flowed as a cloud passed over. There were fields where neat drills of turnips and potatoes and mangolds made a pleasing pattern and there were little cottages that looked so much a part of the land that they seemed to have grown there with the crops. The *Maggie May* carried them past big prosperous homes, fine snug dwellings with roofs of blue slate, and flanked by orchards where the young hard fruit showed up with startling greenness against the dark of the leaves.

Big Bill came up the ladder from the cabin.

"I must say the three of you are looking pleased with yourselves," he said.

Mike scooped the eye out of a potato with the point of his knife. "I wish this could go on for ever."

"What? The potato-peeling, is it?" Big Bill asked.

"No — I mean sailing on the *Maggie May*," Mike said.

"And going to stay with Aunt Sarah," said Essie.

"And having you to take us to the zoo and places," Con said.

Big Bill smiled. He started down the ladder again. "Hurry up with the potatoes, lads — I've got the rabbits skinned and cleaned and ready to go on."

"We won't be five minutes," they promised. "They're just done." Someone else came to hurry them up. Dinny, who had been helping Uncle Pat to do something with the engine, now stumped towards them.

"Are you two going to be all day with that bucket?" he asked sourly. "I'd have a pit of potatoes peeled by this time."

"We're peeling the last of them, Dinny," Con said, placatingly.

"Not so much of the 'Dinny'," he snapped. "It'll be 'Mr Smullen' to the two of you from now on. I'm waiting on that bucket. I've a bit of washing to do, and I'd like to get it done now while I've a minute to spare. It's likely I'll have to be down on me marrow-bones scrubbing and cleaning after you before we get into Dublin."

When the last of the potatoes had been peeled, Dinny took the bucket of dirty water and peelings, tipped it over the side and drew it up filled with clean water. A baby perch was swimming frantically in the bucket. Dinny scooped up the wriggling little thing in his cupped hands and threw it back to join its brothers in the canal. Then he carried the bucket as far as possible from the children and started to wash a shirt with angry vigour.

Con went off to talk to Uncle Pat who was at the tiller. In the confined spot where the skipper stood there was room only for the two of them, so Essie and Mike remained where they were.

All this time, the little pig which Dinny was taking to his friend in Athy had been sleeping contentedly in the sun. Now, unnoticed by anyone, it awakened and rose to its feet. Deciding it would like to stretch its legs, it started off for a brisk trot around the deck, but was soon brought to an abrupt halt by the rope that tethered its hind leg to the ring. Pigs are stubborn beings. They like to get their own way. That little pig wanted to go for a walk, and he was determined that no rope would stop him. He struggled and wriggled madly until finally he managed to break away from his moorings.

It was only in that moment that Mike and Essie realised what was happening.

"Hey, Dinny! Dinny!" Mike jumped to his feet. "Watch out! Look at your little pig!"

Dinny raised his head from the bucket of washing. The pig was careering towards him in a wild scamper. "Go back! Lie down! Hoosh — you'll be drowned!" In an effort to head off the pig, Dinny hopped this way and that, and waved his arms like a windmill. Con raced to his aid, and so did Mike and Essie. Big Bill heard the noise and came up from the cabin. He joined in the chase, and soon the deck was a nightmare of ducking, frightened pig, stamping feet, waving arms and excited shouts. But the little pig eluded them all. It rushed

right over the edge of the boat and into the canal, carrying with it Dinny's clothes-line and shirt.

Dinny was distracted. "Oh, my little pig. Oh, my lovely shirt!" he lamented. "How am I to face the woman in Athy, and her good money's worth of bacon drowned in the canal? And my lovely shirt that had years of wear in it yet — the stuff in it was that strong it would hold the full of itself of water. Oh what will I do at all?"

The little pig was threshing the water, making frantic efforts to keep afloat. The shirt was sinking — one arm waggled sadly on the surface of the canal as if waving goodbye to its owner.

"Oh, if only I could swim!" Dinny moaned. "If only I could swim!"

Con and Mike looked at each other. Without a word and in less time than it takes to tell, they were stripped and diving into the dark green water. With swift strong strokes they swam towards the pig and the shirt.

"I'll tackle the pig, Mike," Con shouted. "Go after the shirt, you."

It was well that Con, who was the better swimmer, took on the harder task, for the little pig struggled like an eel when he tried to grasp it.

"Hold on to her son!" shouted Uncle Pat, who had stopped the engine. "We'll throw you a rope."

The rope was thrown. Con, treading water, managed to tie the end of it around the pig and it was hauled to safety, its grunts and squeals proving that it was not affected in the least by its bath. Mike swam up with the shirt and threw it to Dinny who clutched both his dripping possessions in great thankfulness.

Big Bill and Uncle Pat helped the two boys aboard and hurried them into the cabin for a brisk rub-down. When they came on deck, flushed and tousled-haired, the pig was safely captive in a crate, the shirt was once more flapping in the breeze, and Dinny, very shamefaced and embarrassed looking, was waiting for them. "About that little matter of the drop of tar, lads," he began. "We'll forget about it."

"You're not vexed about it any more, then, Mr Smullen?" Con asked.

"I'm Dinny to you boys," he answered. "And I'm not the type of man to hold a little accident against anyone. Here, shake! You are a powerful pair of swimmers."

The boys were glad to shake hands and be friends.

"All hands on deck for dinner!" shouted Big Bill, coming up the ladder balancing a pile of plates in one hand and carrying the pot of steaming stew in the other. "This will soon put heat into you after your swim."

"And afterwards I'll play 'Red O'Hanlon' on the melodeon, and tell a few stories too," Dinny offered.

And so the evening passed happily in song and story until the *Maggie May* nosed her way into Dublin and came to anchor in Portobello Harbour.

CHAPTER FIVE

UNCLE Pat and Big Bill brought the children to Aunt Sarah's house in Whitechurch Lane. After the confusion and noise of the big streets, they loved Whitechurch Lane. It was a small neat street of houses. The houses were dressed all alike in white lace curtains and green painted doors and railings.

Aunt Sarah had a hundred welcomes for them. She hugged and kissed Con and Essie and declared that she could see a great likeness to her father and mother in them. She had a kiss and a hug for Mike too, and her eyes grew wet when Essie gave her the basket of white heather from Granda and delivered his message.

The children took to Aunt Sarah at once. She was a rosy old woman, round and comfortable, with a top-knot of white hair and a double ration of chins.

When she had chatted a while with Big Bill and Uncle Pat, she excused herself, saying: "Let the children put on the gramophone there and amuse themselves while I wet the tea. I've the table set and all, and I've only to pour the water on the pot. Mr Green will be having tea with us."

"Uncle Pat, who is Mr Green?" Essie whispered when Aunt Sarah had gone into the kitchen.

"He's your aunt's lodger," Uncle Pat explained. "He's a very old man, going on for ninety, and a man of great learning. I believe he was a newspaper man in his day. Now he does nothing but read from morning till night."

Mike thought it must be great to be Mr Green. The three of them felt a little shy of meeting the old scholar, but when he sat down to tea with them they found there was no cause for shyness. There was such kindness in Mr Green's dim brown eyes and such friendliness in his voice, that they were soon chatting to him as if they had known him all their lives. Big Bill found plenty to say to him too, for Mr Green was a well-travelled man and had been in many of the far-off places that Big Bill knew. There was so much talk that it was late when Big Bill and Uncle Pat stood up to go home.

"I'll be here early in the morning to take you to the zoo, lads," Big Bill promised.

"And I'll be along tomorrow evening some time to take you to the pictures," said Uncle Pat.

The three children went to bed happy.

There were only two bedrooms in Aunt Sarah's house. Essie was to sleep with Aunt Sarah, a bed was made for Con on the sofa in the parlour and a stretcher-bed was put up for Mike in Mr Green's room.

No sooner was his head on the pillow than Con was sleeping. Essie chatted for a little while with Aunt Sarah, then her eyelids dropped and she, too, was fast asleep. Mike was restless after Mr Green put out the light and said goodnight to him. Though tired enough from the excitement of the day, he found it hard to sleep. The night noises of the city were partly responsible, but more to blame were the words that kept dancing around in his head, trying to form themselves into a pattern. He had an idea for a poem, and once an idea came it gave him no rest. Always, when he reached this stage in making up a poem, he had to find pencil and paper and write the whole thing down at once in case the words he had struggled so hard to find should be forgotten. At home in Glanaree, Big Bill never minded if he slipped out of his bunk at night, lit the candle in the kitchen and scribbled for a little while. But he could not do that here. And so, while hoping that his poem would stay with him until the morning, he tossed and turned and tried to sleep.

A voice called quietly to him from the bed at the other side of the room, "Are you not sleeping either, Mike?"

"No, Mr Green," Mike answered. "I've been trying to go to sleep but I'm not able."

"In that case" Mr Green said, "we'll turn on the light and read." He switched on the little reading lamp over his bed and reached a thin old arm for his spectacles. "Thank God for books," he went on. "The older I get, the more I value them. Whether I'm lonely by day or sleepless by night, I've only to turn to my books and I find friendship and comfort. Make friends with books, Mike. They'll never fail you."

Mike felt sorry for Mr Green. Though he loved books himself, he felt it would be a sad and lonely thing to have to rely entirely on them for friendship. He raised himself on his elbow and looked across to where the old man lay. "Do you often lie awake reading at night, Mr Green?" he asked.

"Often boy. You know human beings are very like plants and flowers. It's only when they're young and healthy that plants get a good night's rest. Living in the country, you'll have noticed how flowers sleep when they're young. Take the poppy, for instance, and the daisy. When night comes, they tuck their petals snugly in and sleep without stirring till morning."

"Yes," Mike had noticed that.

"But you're not eighty yet, Mike. Why are you so sleepless

tonight? Is your bed not comfortable?"

"It's grand, Mr Green," Mike answered.

"What has you awake, then?"

"I was making up a poem," the boy confessed slowly. "I wish I had a pencil and paper to write it down."

"You'll find a writing-pad and a pen in the top drawer of my bureau," Mr Green told him. "Hop out and get them. You write your poem while I read. I would be most interested to see it when you're finished."

In two minutes Mike was writing away for dear life. When he had finished, he said, "I have it written now, Mr Green." Shyly Mike handed it over. The old man read the lines.

> At times, when I think of the place where You grew,
> I think it a pity that You only knew
> The queer plants and trees and the pathways of sand
> And the dry hungry hills of that strange foreign land,
> With never a taste of the blackberry sweet
> And never a boghole to dabble Your feet.
> The sport that we'd have if You came once again
> And chose for Your birthplace a cottage in Shane!
> It's jumping the bogholes together we'd be
> And eating the griddle-bread hot for our tea,
> And out with a rod after perches and eels,
> And getting a ride on top of the creels.
> I'd show You the nest I found down by the mill
> Where the mother-bird hatches so happy and still.
> I'd show You the hole where the water-rat feeds,
> And how to make whistles from willows and reeds.
> Ah, little Lord Jesus, if You came again
> Would You chose for Your birthplace a cottage in Shane?

56

"Shane is a place that's near us at home," Mike explained. "I wanted to say Glanaree instead of Shane, but I couldn't get it to rhyme."

"Shane does very well," Mr Green said. "Would you let me keep this, Mike? Just for a few days? I'd like to show it to a friend of mine."

"Of course, Mr Green," Mike agreed. "But my handwriting is terrible. And there's a big blot on it. If I was writing at a table, it'd be neater."

"I'm sure my friend will make allowances," the old man said. "I'll tell him you can write much more neatly when you're sitting at a table. And in return for letting me have the loan of your poem, I'm going to give you a present. Do you see that leather-bound book on the top shelf in the corner beside the window? Hand it down to me."

Mike climbed on a chair and took down the book.

Mr Green held it and fondled it as if it were very dear to him. "This book was written over two hundred years ago by a great scholar," he said. "He was a Bog of Allen man, like yourself. He loved the bog and everything about it, and he set down here stories that other people had forgotten — stories of the race of heroes that hunted and fought and lived in the Bog of Allen in days gone by. It's a rare book, Mike, I don't believe there are six copies of it in the world today."

"Oh, but I couldn't take such a book from you, Mr Green," Mike protested. "It must be worth a lot of money."

Mr Green put the book in Mike's hand. "Take it," he said. "I'm giving it to you because I know you'll value it. You love books and you love the bog and you're a poet."

Mike did not know which pleased him more, the book or hearing himself called a poet. He stammered his thanks, but

Mr Green cut him short.

"Into bed with you now," he said, "and no more poem-writing tonight. Remember you've to be up early to get to the zoo in the morning."

Mike got back into bed. He put the book under his pillow and was soon asleep. His dreams that night would not have been so untroubled if he could have foreseen the adventures that awaited him as a result of the present he had received. Nor would Mr Green have read so peacefully into the night if he could have known that the book he had given with such kindness was to lead Mike and others into trouble and danger.

CHAPTER SIX

THEY were at the gate of the zoo by ten o'clock next morning.

Big Bill paid the old man at the turnstile while the children, full of eagerness, peered through the railing.

With maddening slowness, the old man released the turnstile four times. Finally the friends were through and hurrying up the flower-bordered path where peacocks trailing gorgeous feathers stepped disdainfully out of their way and rubber-necked hungry geese came waddling to welcome them.

"Where are the monkeys Big Bill?" Essie said excitedly. "I want to see them — I've been dying to see a monkey ever since I read about the monkey that used to drink coffee."

"You'll see any amount of them in a minute, Essie," Big Bill told her. "Here we are right at their house."

It was a perfect day. The sun shone brightly on the zoo gardens, the water in the lake gleamed with a deep blue, the birds in the aviary sang sweetly. Even the animals seemed to know it was a special occasion, for they did all their best tricks for the children's amusement.

Charlie, the big easy-going chimpanzee, mesmerised them by lighting and smoking the cigarette which a keeper gave him, while Susie, his wife, looked on enviously from her swing and begged with grunts for just one whiff. When greedy Charlie ignored her and puffed away selfishly, she jumped down huffily and waddled to the corner of the cage where she turned her back on all of them and sulked.

"Wait till we see could we get her attention," Big Bill said. He took the big door-key of the cabin out of his pocket and rattled it along the bars of the cage. Susie pricked up her ears. She peeked around over her hunched shoulders and her little eyes brightened with interest in this thing that was making the noise.

"Come on, girl," Big Bill invited. "Come over here and make friends with us." Susie came — but more quickly than any of them expected. With a bound, she was at the bars. Before Big Bill could step back, her black strong fingers had darted out and had wrenched the key from his grasp. Impishly, she waved it in front of his eyes as if to say, "You can whistle for this now." She started to do a slow lumbering dance around the cage, rattling the key on every bar as she went.

"Well!" said Big Bill. "I'm thinking we'll have to climb down the chimney when we get home, Mike."

The children could do nothing but laugh.

"That's all very well," Big Bill said ruefully, "but what am I going to do for the key?"

At last the keeper had an idea. "Wait a minute," he said. He went off, and soon returned with a big padlock and key.

"Come here, Susie," he called. "Look at this." Susie sidled over suspiciously. The keeper took the key out of the padlock, put it back again, then turned it in the lock. He did this several times, while Susie watched with growing interest. Finally the keeper put the key in his pocket.

60

"Now, you try it with your key, Susie," he said. "See if you can do it. I bet you can't."

Thoughtfully, Susie sucked Big Bill's key for a few minutes, then she pushed the key through the bars and tried to fit it into the padlock. The keeper seized the right moment when her fingers were loose on the key to pull it from her grasp. Her howl of rage when she discovered how she had been tricked could have been heard back home in Glanaree. She beat her chest and thumped the floor and roared for vengeance.

By this time Charlie had finished his cigarette. With his leathery thumb, he tapped out the butt carefully on the floor of the cage. With every line of him showing the annoyance he felt at this fuss his mate was creating, he waddled to a pile of sacks in the corner of the cage. He arranged them neatly and got into bed. Before settling himself to rest he gave a last disgusted look at Susie as if to say, "Such tantrums."

Fun though it had been to watch Charlie and Susie, Essie liked the small monkeys better. She loved the mother monkey that was so gentle with her biscuit-coloured wrinkled baby. It was lovely so see how carefully the mother dangled the little thing in the crook of her arm, every two minutes pushing back the egg-sized head and looking down gloatingly as if to say: "Aren't you the beautiful thing!" Seeing the mother's rapture, Essie herself could nearly believe the baby was beautiful, though she had to admit that Con was telling no lie when he said it looked like a withered, bearded little old man that had been lost by the fairies.

They all enjoyed the lions, even though when they entered the lion-house they were nearly deafened by the noise made by a lion and a lioness who were roaring back and forth at each other from separate cages. The lion was a magnificent creature with a long tawny mane that shook with every roar. The lioness was sleek and placid.

She lay happily on the floor of the cage while her two cubs frolicked over her. The noise the two made was ear-splitting.

"What's up with them?" Big Bill asked a keeper.

"Nothing at all," the man answered with a grin. "They carry on like that every morning. The father below is asking questions about the two children and the mother is answering him. If you listen, you'll be able to make out what they're saying."

They listened. Sure enough, by the varying tones of the lions' roars they were able to follow the conversation between the proud papa and mama.

"Gir-rr-rr!" roared father lion. "Are the two children all right?"

"Gr-rr-rr-ow!" answered mother. "Have sense, man. Aren't they here under my eye? I wouldn't let a fly light on them."

"Gir-oo-ooo," the father roared back. "How is Gerald's cold?"

"Gir-ee-ee," the mother assured him. "Grand today. He never sniffed once, and he ate every scrap of his breakfast."

The children, and Big Bill too, could have stayed by every cage for an hour. But there was so much to see — the snarling, snapping wolves, behind their barricade, the slothful crocodiles, the snake that was shedding his skin and was half-in and half-out of a tube of skin that looked like crumpled tissue-paper, the fleecy rabbits, the whiskered fat old sea-lions, the baleful vulture that Mike said reminded him of McFadden, and the exquisite little birds ringed with flaming colour that were as small as butterflies. In the parrot-house they laughed till the tears came, to see the wise-looking parrot tuck his wings into his sides like an old man putting his hands in his pockets and strut up and down the cage, nodding his head with every step as if he were thinking out some problem of great importance. Now and then, he would halt and cock a yellow eye at them hopefully and mutter in his hoarse deep voice: "Scratch poor Poll. Any water? Goodbye."

At length they had to tear themselves away and make for the bus which would take them back to Aunt Sarah's house and dinner.

Con and Mike and Essie felt certain that Dublin had nothing to offer which would compare with the zoo, yet they soon found that each day brought its own delights. There was a visit to the cinema with Uncle Pat and afterwards supper in a café. There was a thrilling climb up a winding stairs right to the top of Nelson's Pillar, from where they were able to look down on a city that seemed to be peopled with toy buses and tiny people. Big Bill took them to the factory behind Marlborough Street. Here they saw dozens of people working happily away among whirring machines that turned the flat sheets of cows' horn into combs and beads. The smell of the hot horn was so bad that Essie had to hold her nose, but she felt it had been well worth while when the kind proprietor gave her a big box of discarded beads, yellow and amber and green and red.

"Make yourself necklaces and beads out of these," he said.

"And you can give me any you have left over," Con said.

"They'll come in handy for an idea I have for a Christmas box."

Before their holiday was over, they were given several presents. Uncle Pat bought Con a splendid torch that sent out a beam like a searchlight, and Big Bill brought both of the boys to an old shop down the quays one day and let them choose a pocket-knife each. The choice fell on what Big Bill called "Two murderous weapons with as many blades as would stock a cutler's shop".

For Essie there was a special present too. After tea one evening Aunt Sarah called her into the bedroom and closed the door.

"Essie child," Aunt Sarah said. "I'm going to give you something I've treasured for fifty years. When I was young, I was nurse to a little girl who was more of an angel than a child, and the poor thing died when she was ten. For a keepsake, her mother gave me little Catherine's work-box. And now I'm going to give it to you."

"Oh, Aunt Sarah!" Essie's face was pink with pleasure.

Aunt Sarah opened the press in the wall and took out something which was wrapped carefully in a clean worn sheet. She unwrapped the sheet and handed Essie the work-box.

Essie gave a gasp of delight. The work-box was lovely — a rosewood casket inlaid with leaves and birds of mother-of-pearl, and with four little feet of silver. Essie just held the box and looked at it.

"Go on, child," Aunt Sarah said. "Turn the key and open it."

When the box was opened, a faint smell of flowers rose from within. It was lined with satin, once white, but now yellowed by age to the colour of old ivory. Every compartment in the box held a treasure. There was a silver thimble which Essie found fitted her perfectly. There was a little gilt scissors in the shape of a stork, its long beak forming the two thin blades, its legs and wing-tips forming the handle. There was a mother-of-pearl needle-case, a silver bodkin and a crochet-hook, a tiny gold pencil, and an inch-tape in a little embroidered case which, Aunt Sarah said, Catherine had made herself. There were spools of silk too, which once upon a time had been bright and vivid, but which now were faded like a waning rainbow.

Essie hardly knew how to thank her aunt. When every treasure had been fondled and admired and returned to its satin nest, Aunt Sarah said, "The sewing silk won't be much use to you, Essie. Just the same, I'd like you to keep it in the box. I'd like to think that Catherine's work-box would go on holding all the things she used to keep in it."

"And it will," Essie promised. "You kept it safe for fifty years and so will I."

Although Mike thought the work-box a lovely present for a girl, and Con a lucky boy to have been given such a fine torch, he felt that his own special present — the book Mr Green had given him — was the best gift of all. He had already dipped into it here and there, and was delighted to discover that one of the stories was about his own townland, Glanaree. Here in Dublin, with so many places to go to and so much to see, he had little time for reading, but he promised himself that it would be the very first story he'd read when he should be back home.

Friday morning came, bringing with it the end of their holiday.

"When you come next year you'll have to stay much longer," Aunt Sarah said when they were leaving.

At the end of Whitechurch Lane, they turned to wave a last goodbye to the little white-haired lady who stood at her green-painted door, smiling and waving. From the window of Mr Green's room a hand was waving too.

The old man leaned on his stick and looked down at the dog stretched listlessly at his feet.

"Lonesome enough we've been these past few days. Eh, Bruss boy?" he said.

"Cheer up, boy," he said. "I wasn't going to tell you at all, because I wanted to give you a pleasant surprise, but sure I can't bear to see you so sad." He bent lower, and whispered. "They're coming home, Bruss boy! They'll be home today!"

Bruss's head rose with a jerk. An excited quiver ran through him right down to his tail. With a bound he was on his feet and running wildly around the yard, frightening the life out of the squawking hens.

"Woof! Woof! Woof! Woof! Woof! Woof!" barked Bruss, which being roughly translated, meant, "Hurrah! Three cheers! They're coming! Rabbits for Bruss! Nice cool swims for Bruss! Nice bits from Essie's plate for Brussie!"

The noise brought Mrs Byrne to the door.

"What in the world is wrong?" she asked. "Is he gone out of his mind, or what?"

"No, girl," Granda said. "It's only that he's delighted because the children are coming home today."

Up in Glanaree House a scene of far greater excitement was taking place.

Along a tunnel which burrowed from the cellar to the heart of the rath, McFadden was stumbling. The roof of the tunnel was so low that the long gaunt hermit was bent almost double. His haste and excitement made him trip at every second step. But he hardly felt the sharp stones that cut into his knees every time he tripped, nor did he heed the blood that dripped from his torn and bruised hands.

The man was like one in a trance. He was trembling. His red-rimmed eyes glittered. Over and over again, he whispered gloatingly: "At last! At last I have it! At last it's mine!"

He reached the mouth of the tunnel and crawled out into the dank cellar. Light filtered through a small dirty window near the roof and showed dimly a number of crates that stood around the walls.

McFadden straightened himself.

"Tobin!" he called hoarsely. "Tobin! Come here!"

The cellar door opened and McFadden's servant came through, a swarthy, thick-set man, low-browed and coarse-featured.

"I'm here," the man answered in a surly tone. "What do you want? If it's to start digging again after the way you had me at it all last night you're —." He stopped short suddenly, struck by the expression on McFadden's face.

"I found it," McFadden said. "At last I found it. Didn't I tell you many times during these past few months that we were near it? When you grew discouraged and wanted to give up, like the cowardly fool you are, didn't I persuade you to persevere a little longer? Didn't I say that our years of work would be rewarded? Well, I was right! It's mine at last!"

Tobin, who had been staring dumbly at his master, now spoke. "It's *ours*," he corrected him. "Half of it is mine. I've worked as hard as you for it."

McFadden's eyes became crafty. "Of course, Tobin," he said, and there was false wheedling in his voice. "Of course, you'll get your share — that was the bargain. But we have plenty of work to do, still. Now you can unpack the crates and we'll set up the laboratory." His vice rose higher and higher in his excitement. "Think of it, Tobin! Molten gold...the lovely shining metal seething into the crucibles ...flowing in a pure glittering stream into the moulds...setting into heavy solid bars of bright gleaming gold! Gold, Tobin...gold!" His voice ended almost on a scream.

Tobin glanced quickly up at the window. "Shut up, you fool!" he said warningly. "Do you want someone to hear you? Maybe you want to tell the workers out there on the bog all about it."

McFadden quietened. "The louts!" he said with contempt. "The stupid louts! For twenty years I've held off their curiosity and their attempts to pry into my secret. Soon now I'll be able to get away from them and from this hole of a place. With my brains and with the wealth that will be mine, I'll live royally, Tobin. I'll be a king among men."

He laughed — a horrible whinnying laugh.

"I shall be King, Tobin, and you shall be my prime minister!"

"Not if I know it," Tobin said sourly. "You can get yourself crowned King, for all I care, but I'm striking out on my own. I've my own ideas about the way I'm going to spend my share. And now I want to see it. I want to know how much is coming to me. Is it all there?"

"All of it, Tobin!" McFadden exulted. "All that I ever promised you — every ounce of it. Come and see for yourself."

He turned and, crouching low, re-entered the tunnel. Tobin followed him.

CHAPTER SEVEN

WHEN Con and Essie got up on the Monday morning after their return from Dublin, they found their father in the kitchen. He was dressed in his oldest clothes.

"Are you not going to work today, father?" Essie asked, sitting down to her breakfast.

"No, love," her father answered. "I'm taking the week off to draw out the turf. I walked up to our bank yesterday evening to see how the turf was getting on and it's bone-dry. I'm taking you with me, Con."

"Hurrah!" Con shouted. He loved the long days on the bog when he worked like a man and his father treated him as his equal.

"You can yoke up Neddeen as soon as you're finished your breakfast," his mother told him. "Big Bill and Mike will be giving us a hand. They're bringing the jennet. Between the four of you, you should have every sod of it drawn out in a few days."

"And then we'll draw out Big Bill's turf," Jem Byrne said.

"I will carry down their dinner to them, mother," Essie suggested, knowing the kind of appetite they always got when working on the bog.

When they reached the turf-bank, which was about a mile from the cottage, they found Big Bill and Mike already working. Several loads of turf were drawn out to the side of the road. When all the turf had been drawn out, it would be built into a weatherproof clamp. There was no room at home in the yard for the turf. The clamp was always left at the roadside, and a load drawn home as it was needed.

Under the bright sun, they worked happily all morning. They did not realise how hard they had been working or how hungry they were until Big Bill sighted Essie coming up the road, a big basket in one hand and a can of milk in the other.

"Down tools now, lads," he called to Mike and Con. "I see our dinner coming. Start the fire and set a can of water to boil for the tea."

"I'll run for the water, Mike," Con said. "You get the fire going." His long legs carried him swiftly over the heather to where a little stream of fresh water gurgled its happy way. When he returned, Mike had the fire going with a big flat sod at each side for hobs. The blackened can was balanced on the hobs, and by the time Essie came up, the water was boiling merrily.

"What did you bring us, Essie?" Con asked as he took the basket from her.

"There's potato cakes," Essie told him, "and fresh griddle-bread and rashers, and the cold meat that was left since yesterday for Big Bill and father, and rice in the little pie-dish for yourself and Mike."

"When they had eaten, they settled themselves for half an hour's rest before returning to work. Jem Byrne and Big Bill lay on their backs in the heather, and contentedly watched the smoke curl up from their well-earned pipes. The boys strolled over to the shade of a big rowan tree, where Con started to amuse himself by plaiting reeds for a whip and Mike, taking

72

Mr Green's book out of his pocket, began to read.

"I don't know how you content yourself with your nose stuck in a book," Con grumbled. "Can't you come on and jump bog-holes, or something?"

"Whisht, will you?" Mike said. "I'm reading a story about this very spot. Leave me in peace, can't you?" Presently he sat up excitedly. "Listen, Con," he said. "It says here that Fionn Mac Cumhaill had a fort in Glanaree one time and that he lived in it up to the time when Gráinne ran away on him."

"Who was Gráinne?" Con asked, plaiting away at his whip.

Mike explained. "Gráinne was a lovely princess, the daughter of Cormac Mac Airt, the King of Tara. Her father promised Fionn he could marry her; but on the very day they were to be married, she ran away with Diarmuid."

"Why did she do that?" Con wanted to know. "Wasn't he the champion hero of them all?"

"He was — but Diarmuid was a hero too. Besides, Fionn was an old man at this time and Diarmuid was young. Anyway, Gráinne was in love with Diarmuid. Fionn was mad when she ran away and made a show of him like that. He set out after the two of them and chased them through the length and breadth of Ireland."

"Did he ever catch up on them?"

"No," Mike said. "He followed them for many a long day, but they always got away from him, for the people of Ireland helped them. It wasn't that the people were against Fionn — indeed, they thought the world of him for his bravery and fine deeds. But they were sorry for Diarmuid and Gráinne. So at long last Fionn gave up the chase and came home."

"What happened then, Mike?"

"I'm just coming to that part. I'll read it out for you." Mike read aloud, while the bees in the gorse, drunk with honey, hummed drowsily from blossom to blossom, and Con bound the thong of plaits into a handle of strong reeds. "So Fionn returned to his fort in Glanaree, and a great anger came on him when he looked around at the splendour he had prepared for Gráinne. He looked around at the heavy bracelets and collars and girdles and brooches, at the sets of drinking vessels and banqueting plates and the dishes large enough to hold a roast calf, all of them made from pure gold. Then Fionn swore a mighty oath that since Gráinne had turned her back on all these splendours, no other woman would ever wear the golden ornaments and no other person would eat from the golden dishes nor drink from the golden goblets. 'I will leave this place,' said Fionn, 'and neither I nor one of my followers will ever again set foot in it.' And so it was done. The fort of Glanaree became empty and desolate. Grass grew high around that door where there had been such coming and going, and the wild things of the earth made their home in the banqueting hall. But Fionn and his followers were seen there no more. In later years, a king built himself a castle on the site of Fionn's fort. He, too, went his way, and his castle fell into ruins. No trace was ever found of the golden store which had been fashioned for Gráinne. Some say that Fionn had the gold melted into coins to buy arms for his men when he led them to battle against the men of Connacht. Others say that the treasure is buried deep in the earth where no man will ever find it."

The boys were silent for a minute when the story was ended. "That was a good story," Con said then. "I wouldn't have any objection at all to reading if all the books were about people being chased and things like that." He neatened

74

off the handle of his whip. To try it out, he slashed the heads from a few tufts of bog-cotton.

In Mike's brain a great idea was being born. "Listen, Con," he said slowly, and there was a quiver of excitement in his voice. "The ruined castle and Fionn's fort — where there was a fort there was always a rath. A castle and a rath...where in Glanaree have we the two things together?"

Con saw what Mike was driving at. "You mean that the Big House is the place in the story?"

Mike nodded. "Suppose Fionn never melted down the goblets and things? Suppose he buried them before he left the fort and that they have been lying there all these years?"

"And what about it?" Con said. "It isn't likely that we two would ever find them."

"It isn't," Mike agreed. "But maybe somebody else would, McFadden, for instance. That's his secret! That's what brought him here in the first place — to look for Fionn's treasure. He got on the track of it, somehow."

Con whistled. His excitement was now as great as Mike's. "You're right! You're right, Mike! That's why he wouldn't make friends with anyone. That's why he chased everyone who went near the place."

"It explains everything," Mike said. "Even that scraping sound we heard in the rath the day we were picking strawberries. Do you remember it?"

"I do. I thought it was a rabbit."

"I had my doubts, Con. I knew no rabbit ever burrowed with metal. Well, what are we going to do? Will we tell anyone?"

Con thought for a second. "We won't," he decided. "We'll keep it a secret. We'll do a bit of scouting around

McFadden's place to see if we can discover anything. If we tell them at home they'll say we're only dreaming and they'll forbid us to go near the Big House. Better not say a word to anyone."

"Won't we even tell Essie?" Mike did not like Essie to be left out of things.

"Better not," Con said. "She'd be no use and we won't tell Granda either. He's dead set against us going near McFadden's place. This is a secret between the two of us."

They shook hands on it.

Just then Big Bill's voice hailed them. "Come on, lads," he called. "Back to work. Or are you going to sit there talking all day?"

The boys jumped to their feet.

"We're coming," Mike cried.

"Not a word," Con warned him.

The hours wore on. The work was well divided. Big Bill loaded the carts. Mike was in charge of the jennet, Con in charge of the ass. As the carts were loaded, the boys guided their charges down the turf-bank and over the little bridge of planks that spanned the bog-stream which ran by the roadside. Here Jem Byrne was waiting to unload the turf and clamp it. Then back up the bank again with Neddeen and the jennet for another load. They were tired enough when the church bell rang, telling them that the day's work had ended.

Essie and her mother had returned from the town by the time they got home. Mrs Byrne had a steaming stew for which they were very ready.

Tired though they were, the boys decided to start their scouting that very night, so when supper was over they slipped out of the house and started off for McFadden's place.

"Mind you," Mike said as they went, "we may be all wrong. Maybe there was no truth in that story we read. It was true about Diarmuid and Gráinne, of course, and about Fionn chasing them."

"Why wouldn't the rest of it be true, then?" Con demanded."

"You couldn't be sure," Mike answered. "You know the way it is about a thing that happened long ago. First it's told just the way it happened. Then as the years go on, one person adds one bit and another bit. Maybe that bit about Fionn's treasure was added on, though I don't think it was."

"It would be easy enough to find out," Con pointed out. "You could write to Mr Green and ask him if the story is true. He'd know, for sure."

"I'll do that," Mike said. "There's another thing I want to ask him too. I was thinking that if the story *is* true and if McFadden is really on the right track of the treasure, maybe he has every right to it. Maybe we shouldn't be interfering with him. After all, finders are keepers."

"Not when it's a case of buried treasure," Con said. "I can tell you that for certain, because only last night I heard Granda telling how Uncle Pat once found an old spearhead in the bog when he was cutting turf. He wasn't let keep it. Anything you find like that belongs to the whole nation and has to be sent up to the Museum. He got a reward of some kind. Not very much, though. Granda says the reward depends on the value of what you find."

"If that's the case, the reward you'd get for finding Fionn's treasure would be worth having!" Mike exclaimed. "Not that I could see McFadden being satisfied with just the reward.

No fear of him sending the whole lot up to the Museum."

"You could ask Mr Green, just the same," said Con. "And while we're waiting for him to answer, we will keep an eye on McFadden and try to find out what he's up to."

Thinking it wiser not to make straight for the Big House, they had taken a roundabout way and the light was fading by the time they came out at the rath behind the orchard. Con gripped Mike's arm. "Look!" he whispered excitedly. "There's McFadden going off for a walk with his dog." Sure enough, through the dusk Mike could see the long shambling figure setting off across the bog, with the big dog trotting behind him.

"Now's our chance to creep close to the house and find out if there's anything to be seen through the windows," Con went on. "There will be nobody there but the servant and we can run if he sees us. Are you game?"

Of course Mike was game. They tip-toed cautiously down the boreen, along the road and up to the front gate. There was no light in any of the windows. The gate was locked and they had to climb it, dropping quietly on the grass-grown avenue. Here they listened intently for a moment to make sure Tobin had not heard them. But no sound came from the Big House and, cautiously, they began to advance. As the avenue was in full view of the windows, they slipped into the shrubbery, and made their slow cautious way from bush to bush. The neglected shrubbery was a jungle of high wiry weeds and clinging bramble, and they had to force a way for themselves. Each time a dry twig snapped underfoot, or a branch rustled loudly and protestingly as they pushed it aside, they stood and listened for the sound of an opening door and a threatening voice. But Tobin evidently was not on the watch tonight, for they succeeded in reaching the house without disturbing him.

At first they found little to reward their pains. They peered in through the ground-floor windows in the front of the house, and saw nothing but a few sticks of dilapidated furniture standing ghostly and grim in the faint light. They went around to the back. They found nothing of interest there either — an untidy bedroom and a littered kitchen that had a cold dreary look, as if a decent meal had never been cooked in it.

"We'll go," Mike whispered. "There's nothing to be seen here. Besides, the servant might pounce on us at any minute. Or McFadden himself might come back and catch us. We'd better be going."

"Wait a minute." Con became tense. "Listen!"

From somewhere beneath their feet came a mysterious sound, the sound of something heavy and cumbersome being dragged along. The noise seemed to come from the direction of a small weed-choked incline that sloped down to a tiny cellar window.

The boys looked at each other. "Come on," said Con.

As quietly as they could, they scrambled down the incline. Bending down, they pushed aside the nettles and dock that screened the little window, and rubbed away some of the dirt that caked it. But no matter how hard they looked, they could see nothing because of the darkness inside.

Suddenly Con remembered the torch in his pocket. He held it close to the window and its searching beam lit up a scene that made the boys gasp in wonder. The cellar was littered with all kinds of queer-looking objects that had obviously been taken from the empty packing-cases that lay around.

"What would they be for?" Con whispered.

"I don't know," Mike answered. "They look like the kind of things scientists use for making experiments."

"Maybe McFadden isn't after the treasure at all, then," Con said. "Maybe he's only a scientist who's carrying out some experiment or other."

Mike thought this possible too. At the same time he was doing his best to memorise the queer objects so as to describe them in his letter to Mr Green and find out their use.

Con sent the torch-beam travelling slowly around the cellar. "Look, Mike," he said. "Look at that hole in the wall — over there to the right. It looks like the opening to a tunnel."

So absorbed were the boys that all this time they never noticed that the dragging noise had been growing more distinct. Now it was brought abruptly to their attention. As they stared at that hole in the wall, a figure appeared in it — the crouching figure of Tobin. In one hand he carried a lantern which he held before him. The other hand grasped a rope at which he strained and pulled and which seemed to be attached to some heavy object.

"Put out the torch, Con!" Mike whispered. Con switched off the torch. But he was too late. Tobin had seen that bright beam, so much stronger than the light of the lantern he carried. It did not take him long to realise the meaning of the light — that he was being watched. With a muttered curse, he dropped the rope, picked up a heavy stick and made quickly for the cellar door. It took Con and Mike even less time to realise their danger. They were up that incline and scurrying around to the avenue with the speed of a hare being chased by a greyhound. Down the avenue they sped. They had almost reached the gate when Tobin opened the front door and rushed down the avenue after them. The grey dusk was not thick enough to hide the forms of the boys as they clambered up the gate. In his rage Tobin threw the heavy stick. It caught Mike on the shoulder just as he was getting over the top of the gate, and knocked him heavily to the other side. Con jumped down safely. He bent over his chum who lay without stirring.

"Are you hurt, Mike?" he asked anxiously. Luckily, Mike was not badly hurt, only badly shaken. He was breathless from the fall and from the sudden pain of the blow.

"I'll — I'll be all right in a minute," he said.

Con glanced over his shoulder. Tobin was almost at the gate. He was fumbling in his pocket for the key.

"Come on, Mike!" Con urged. "He's on top of us! He'll catch us! Get up and make a run for it."

With an effort, Mike got to his feet. Tobin had reached the gate now and was fitting the key in the lock. The vindictive look on the man's face and the blood-curdling threats he was uttering gave back to Mike the wind that had been knocked out of him, and made him forget for the moment his aching shoulder. He made a dash for the road, and Con did the same. With thumping hearts and bursting lungs the boys raced through the deepening dusk. The heavy feet of Tobin pounded after them. Had it been daytime, they would have found it easy to escape him, for they could have taken to the bog, where there were paths known only to themselves. But in this dim light, the bog was a dangerous place, and so they had to keep to the road.

"Are we gaining on him?" Con said. The speed at which they were running, coming after the hard day's work, was beginning to tell, even on him.

"Don't ...know," Mike gasped. "Keep...on..."

They kept on, and at last they had the satisfaction of hearing those heavy feet slow down, stop, and then become fainter and fainter as Tobin, having given up the chase, turned back to the Big House. Only when they felt themselves safe did they drop down on the grassy margin at the roadside.

"That was a close one!" Con said when he had recovered his breath. "Did you get a bad blow on the shoulder, Mike?"

Mike swung his arm gingerly. "It hurts a bit," he admitted.

"You're lucky you didn't get it on the head."

"And we're twice as lucky McFadden didn't come home with the dog while we were at that little window. I bet they'll board it up after this."

"It won't do them any good," Con said grimly. "I've made up my mind I'm going to find out what's going on in that house if it's the last thing I do."

"Same here," Mike vowed.

They set out for home, and were so taken up with talking of their adventure that they had reached Big Bill's cabin almost before they knew it.

"See you tomorrow on the bog," Mike called, as he turned in at the gate.

"Don't forget the letter to Mr Green," Con warned.

Mike did not forget it. Tired though he was, he wrote the letter before he went to bed, and put it in the pocket of his jacket. "I'll watch for Bill Casey when he's cycling along the road with the post tomorrow," he told himself. "He'll post it for me. Mr Green will have it on Wednesday. Maybe I'd have an answer by the end of the week."

82

CHAPTER EIGHT

GRANDA was waiting at the gate for them when they came home from work on Friday evening. "Go in and see what Essie and I got for your supper," he said. "It's just for Mike and you, Con."

When the boys went into the kitchen, Mrs Byrne was putting the treat on the table — a bowl of mushrooms prepared in their favourite way, and the boys though pleased were uncomfortable.

Since Monday, they had had a guilty feeling that perhaps it was mean to be keeping Essie out of their secret. Her generosity about the mushrooms increased this feeling. They did not feel so bad about not telling Granda. Although they had let him into many a secret in the past and had always found him ready for a bit of fun, they knew that this time it was different. He would think interfering with McFadden a dangerous business and he would be against it.

Jem Byrne looked up from his place. "I want you to give me a hand in the workshop tonight, Con," he said. "There's that turf-harrow for Tommy Murphy to be finished. I've been promising it to him for the past three weeks."

"Here's another lad who'll give you a hand," Big Bill said. "Mike will be on his own tonight, as I have to go into the town. He can help you, and it will keep him from being lonesome till I get back."

"Good," Jem Byrne said. "Between us we'll have it finished in next to no time."

At any other time, both boys would have been delighted to help in the workshop. This evening, they were not too pleased with the idea. They had been hoping to do another bit of scouting. Since Monday, they had not had a chance to go near the Big House. They had been kept busy in the bog all day, and each evening something had happened to prevent them going out together. On Tuesday, Uncle Pat had come to spend the night. On Wednesday Big Bill had taken Mike off to visit a friend on the other side of the bog, and on Thursday Mrs Byrne had taken it into her head to make Con take a bath in the big wash-tub and go to bed early. However, they had to make the best of it. And anyway, as Mike pointed out later, there wasn't much use in going ahead with the adventure until they heard from Mr Green. His answer to the questions would give them an idea of what they should do.

"I'm afraid we'll have to leave the rest of the turf till Monday," Big Bill announced when he called for Mike that night. "While I was in the town tonight I heard of a man over in Barnalea who's shutting down his shop. He has a lot of delf and stuff that he wants to sell off, and I thought I'd go over and have a look at it."

"That suits me all right," Jem Byrne said. "I've plenty of work here to keep me going. And I'm sure the boys will have no objection to a holiday from the turf. They're after putting in a good hard week's work."

The boys had no objections at all. Essie was pleased too. She had missed them all the week.

When morning came, Mrs Byrne had a plan for them. "You

ought to go up to the commons and see if you could gather me a good big basket of mushrooms," she said. "I think I will make some ketchup."

"There's still two bottles of the ketchup you made last year up there, mother." Essie pointed to the top of the dresser.

Mrs Byrne reached up and took down the bottles. She looked at them doubtfully and then shook her head. "I'd be afraid to use it, Essie. It might have gone sour. It would be safer to throw it out."

"Put the bottles here, mother." Con held out the basin of food he was carrying to the hens. I'll empty them for you."

Con carried out the basin and set it down. At that moment, Mike came through the gate. "What's in the bottles?" he wanted to know. Con told him.

"Don't waste it," Mike said. "Pour it over the hen's food."

Con hesitated. "Would it do them any harm, Mike?"

"What harm could it do them? Think of all the queer things hens eat — gravel and snails and the like. The ketchup will only fatten them."

"Maybe you're right," Con agreed. He pulled the corks from the bottles and emptied them over the mash. The hens seemed to like the stuff. They fell on the food greedily. As they pecked and picked they uttered little gluttonous cluckings of delight.

"Mother wants the three of us to go to the commons for mushrooms," Con told his friend.

"A good idea," Mike agreed with enthusiasm. "Come on and we'll get the basket out of the workshop."

In the workshop they were startled by a wail of horror.

"It's mother!" Con said. He raced in the direction of the cry, followed closely by Mike and Jem Byrne. In the kitchen, they collided with Granda draped in a quilt. The old man had been enjoying a long lie in bed until Mrs Byrne's cry had startled him from his slumbers.

"What is it?" he quavered.

"It's Mary!" Jem Byrne rushed to the kitchen door. "She's out in the yard. I think she must have fallen or something."

His wife had not fallen, but she looked as if at any moment she might. With Essie beside her she was standing in the middle of the yard looking wildly and unbelievingly at the flock of fowl that had been the pride of her life. No one could be proud of them now. The creatures staggered and stumbled about the yard as if their leg-bones were made of rubber. Several of them lay where they had fallen, unable to rise.

"My hens!" Mrs Byrne wailed. "My beautiful hens!"

One horrified glance, and Mike and Con felt their hearts drop like leaden weights. Aghast, they looked at each other. "The ketchup!"

"But what's the matter with the hens?" Jem Byrne asked. "What's after happening to them?"

"It's the plague," Granda said, and there was fear in his voice. "Heaven between us and all harm! It's the plague — and we'll be lucky if it doesn't spread to every living creature on the bog."

Con and Mike looked at each other again. Together, they started to confess.

"It isn't the plague they have —"

"It's the ketchup —"

"It was my fault —"

"No, I poured it on the mash —"

Their faces burned and they stammered under the battery of four pairs of eyes.

86

Jem Byrne's face grew stern. "What's all this?" he demanded.

In a small guilty voice, Con told how he had pepped up the hen's breakfast.

"It was my fault, Mrs Byrne," Mike said guiltily. "I made him do it. I said it wouldn't do them any harm."

Jem Byrne looked at his wife. With a set despairing face she was looking at her stricken fowl. Her face crumpled suddenly and she put her apron to her eyes. "What will we do at all?" she said. "What's going to become of us?"

Miserably, Con and Mike swallowed hard. They could understand Mrs Byrne's distress. Like most of the Glanaree women, she relied on the sale of fowl and eggs for clothing for the family. With her flock gone she had no way of buying the winter clothes they all needed.

There was a sudden gasping sound from Granda. They all looked quickly at him, thinking that the calamity had brought on a stroke. Granda was doubled up, not with pain, but with laughter. He was actually laughing, breathlessly, hysterically, and tears of laughter were running down his cheeks into his beard.

"Granda!" There was incredulous reproach in Mrs Byrne's voice.

"You're fretting over nothing, Mary girl," he said weakly. "The hens are not sick — they're only *drunk!* It's the truth," he went on in answer to their stares. "Keep ketchup for a year and it turns into wine. It went to the creatures' heads. I saw the very same thing happen to a pig we had when I was a boy. You'll find the hens will be all right. When they sleep it off, they'll be as right as rain."

"Is that the truth, Granda?" Mrs Byrne asked quickly,

hardly daring to believe.

"Look at them for yourself and you'll see I'm right," the old man answered.

They all looked again at the fowl...at the pullets that were lying on the ground waving their legs with a slow cycling motion...at the fine young cockerels that were stumbling feebly around as if looking for some place to lay their aching heads, at the fat laying hens that were hunching themselves up in the queerest attitudes, with every feather standing on end, and with their beaks opening now and then on a high thin note of surprise like the cheep of a newly hatched chick.

There was no doubt about it, the hens were hopelessly drunk. Mike looked at Essie, Granda looked at Con, Mrs Byrne looked at her husband. They all started to laugh. They laughed so long and so loudly that they nearly frightened the hens back into their sober senses.

◆

The commons was a wide flat stretch of grazing land that lay half-way between the cottage and the village of Glanaree. When the children started out the sky was covered with little frothy white clouds, but soon a shaft of sunlight cleared them away as cleanly as a spoon skims the froth from boiling jam, and by the time they reached the stile leading into the commons the bog was roofed with unbroken blue.

"Come on, lads!" Con raced before them across the tufted grass. "We'll try the far field first and when we've that cleaned we'll come back to this one."

They carried two baskets, a large one for the platters, the big flat juicy mushrooms which would be made into ketchup,

and a smaller basket for cuppeens, the little white buttons which Mrs Byrne would stew for them in milk. They found plenty of both kinds shining like pale stars in the long grass, and the baskets were more than half-filled when they came back to the first field.

"We'll have a rest now," Essie suggested. "Come on and we'll play a game of jacks. Will you play, Con?"

"Not me. Jacks is a silly game. You're always wanting to play jacks."

"You're saying that because I always beat you," Essie said, and it was true for her. There wasn't one in Glanaree who was her match at jacks. "You never won once."

"Who wants to play anyway?" Con retorted. "I'm going to see are the cherries ripe." He ran off towards the wild cherry tree which grew in the corner of the field near the road.

"Play jacks with me, Mike," Essie pleaded.

"Just the one game then," Mike agreed. He was no better at jacks than Con, but he didn't mind being beaten. He pulled up the grass to make a shorn patch on which to play, and Essie took out of her pocket five smooth jack-stones. They started to play. Without a fault, Essie got through her one-sers, two-sers, three-sers, four-sers, knicky-knacky, leave and take, skim-the-schooner, lick-the-place, crack-jack, no-crack, buttermilk, and bob-the-breast. Mike got stuck in his two-sers and couldn't get out of them. He rumpled his red thatch. "I can't make it out," he said ruefully. "My hand is twice as big as yours and yet the jacks won't stay on it."

"You don't hold it right," Essie told him. "Look, this way." She held out her little hand, palm downwards, and showed him how the fingers should be held stiffly together and bent backwards a little so as to make a hollow on which the jacks would rest. "Try it again, Mike."

"Hey, Mike! Mike!" Con's excited yell interrupted them. "A letter for you! Bill Casey is after throwing it across the hedge to me." Mike jumped to his feet and saw the postman remount his bicycle and ride away with a wave of the hand for all three of them. Con was racing across the field with a letter which he waved wildly.

"It'll be the answer from Mr Green," he cried.

Mike took the letter. He was as excited as Con.

"What's Mr Green writing to you about, Mike?" Essie asked.

The boys looked at each other.

"Tell her," Mike said. "Let Essie into the secret."

Con hesitated.

Essie looked hurt. "Well, aren't you the mean pair! You have a secret and you never told me."

"Arrah, tell her, Con," Mike urged. "Essie won't let it out."

Con gave way. "Do you promise you won't tell anyone?

Not even Granda?"

"Not even Granda. I promise."

"Tell her while I read the letter." Mike tore open the envelope, and Con told Essie the story of Fionn's treasure and the adventure into which their suspicions of McFadden had led them. He had finished long before Mike had read the letter.

"Well, what does Mr Green say?" Con asked impatiently. "Hurry up and tell us." But Mike read on as if he were deaf. Con was feeling that he could cheerfully shake him when at last he came to the end of the long letter and looked up, his eyes shining. He handed the letter to Essie. "Read it out, Essie," he said.

Essie read it out, stammering a little because some of the words were new to her and because Mr Green's handwriting was so spidery and shaky.

> *My dear Mike,*
>
> *Thank you for your letter which I hasten to answer. Before I deal with your questions, it may interest you to hear the fate of the poem which you so kindly lent me. I showed it to my friend, who is the editor of a monthly magazine. As you requested, I told him that you were capable of much better handwriting and that the blots were due to the poem having been written in bed at one o'clock in the morning. The apologies were unnecessary, as my friend did not notice either the handwriting or the blots. He gave all his attention to the poem itself, which he thought very good — so good in fact that he intends to publish it. He will be writing to you himself in the course of a day or two.*

Essie looked up from the letter. "Oh, Mike! Your poem is going to be printed in a magazine!" Pleasure and excitement made her face only one shade less scarlet than Mike's. "Con, isn't it great?"

"It's powerful," Con agreed. "But what else is in the letter? Go on and read what he says about the treasure." Essie read on.

I am glad you find Lays and Legends of Allen *so interesting. I knew you would like it. You ask me if there is any truth in the story of Fionn's buried treasure. Quite frankly, I do not think so. In all my life I have met only one person who believed that story, and as he — poor creature! — was a lunatic, though a gentle harmless one, his opinion was not to be taken seriously. Although it is now more than twenty years since I knew this man, your question brings the whole matter vividly to my mind. It was before I retired from newspaper work. I was working late in my office one night when I was told that an old man wished to see me. I had him brought in — a frail old man who seemed very distressed. From his first words, I saw he was a gentleman and a scholar. He said to me he had been robbed and that he had come to appeal to me for help. I said his best plan would be to seek the aid of the police. He said he had done so, but that the police had refused to believe his story. Personally, when I heard what he had to say, I could not blame them, for his story was so fantastic that no sane person could regard it as anything but the ravings of a madman. Briefly, it boiled down to this. He had discovered, so he said, an ancient Irish manuscript which gave, in a most difficult code, a clue to the whereabouts of the buried treasure of Fionn Mac Cumhaill. With the help of an assistant, he had succeeded after several years' work in decoding part of the manuscript, the least important part. They were just about to start work on the remainder, when the assistant disappeared, taking with him not only the precious manuscript but also a considerable sum of money which the old scholar had kept locked in a safe and which he believed nobody knew of. As I say, the story sounded very fantastic to me, but I was sorry for the old fellow because it was plain that he believed every word of it. He became so excited and upset during the telling of it, and was so exhausted when he had finished that I thought it best to humour him by pretending to believe it and by promising to help to track down the assistant by publishing a description of him in my paper. I remember the old man described him as 'a long, lean, foxy rogue'. When at length my visitor rose to go, he tottered and fell back into his chair. It was then I realised he was a dying man. He gave me the address of his home and I brought him there. It was a miserable room in a mean back street. That night he died. During the following week I made enquiries and found that the poor fellow was a scholar who had lived for his books, for he was quite alone in the world. I could not find any foundation for his story. No one had ever heard of the manuscript of which he spoke. As for the money which he said had been stolen from him, this could have existed only in his imagination, for he was known to have lived in real poverty. The 'lean, long and foxy' description did seem to fit a man who, I was told, used to visit him frequently and spend long hours with him, but as this man was a highly respected and well-known professor, one could not imagine him stealing money and manuscripts. I tried to get in touch with the professor whose name, if I remember rightly, was MacDonald, but I found he had left the country a short time before to take up a teaching post some place abroad. No; I am afraid the manuscript and the money and the theft were all a kind of dream, and that the old man was, as everyone who knew him told me, a little mad. I also fear that you will be setting out on a wild-goose chase if you start looking for Fionn's treasure. If there had been such a treasure, it would have been found long before now.*

Essie interrupted herself and looked up from the letter. "There you are," she said. "You and your great secret! The two of you went prowling around that house and took all that risk over something that never was there at all. Mr Green says so, and he ought to know."

Con looked at his sister in scorn. "You must be blind as a bat, Essie, if you don't see that this letter gives us clear proof that we were right in our guess. Does Mr Green know anything about McFadden and the way he's been carrying on down here? Did he see what Mike and myself saw the other evening? I bet if he did he'd believe in Fionn's treasure all right. What do you say, Mike?"

Mike nodded. His face was tense and his eyes were

LIMERICK CITY LIBRARY

dancing. "I'd say you're right, Con. The old man who called to Mr Green's office wasn't raving at all."

Essie looked from one to the other of them in bewilderment.

Con gave an exclamation of impatience. "It's plain to me, Essie! Mr Green says it's just over twenty years since the old man came to tell him he was after being robbed. Didn't you hear Granda saying the other day that he'd always remember the spring of 1924 because two things happened that April — he broke his leg on the way from the fair of Athy, and McFadden bought Glanaree House? Well, that was just twenty years ago, too. Another thing — that professor fellow was long and lean and foxy. Where would you get anything longer or leaner of foxier than McFadden?"

"But Mr Green says the professor's name was MacDonald," Essie pointed out.

"It would be easy for him to change his name," Mike told her. "And what would he be living on all these years but the money he stole from the old man? You know yourself he never works. McFadden is MacDonald. Wait till you read the rest of the letter — especially the very last bit."

With growing excitement, Essie read on.

> *And now for the answers to your two questions. Number one: Treasure trove is the property of the state and must be handed up, and the finder receives a reward. Number two: The articles you describe seem very like the apparatus (crucibles, etc) used by goldsmiths in melting gold and other precious metals.*

The letter concluded with good wishes for all three

children and the hope that Mike would write soon again.

"Now, are you still thinking the risk we took was for nothing?" demanded Con when Essie had finished reading.

"No," Essie had to admit. "It seems you were right. McFadden must have spent those twenty years trying to decode the manuscript."

"And now he has it!" Mike concluded. "He must have found the treasure or he wouldn't be getting ready to melt it down. Well, what are we going to do?" He sat back on his heels and looked at the other two.

"I think you should go straight to the police and have himself and Tobin arrested," Essie said.

Con gave a short laugh. "What do you think the police would say if we went and told them McFadden is planning to melt down Fionn's hidden treasure? They'd never believe us. We'd only be laughed at, the same as they laughed at the poor old fellow that McFadden robbed."

Mike agreed. "You're right there, Con. The trouble is, grown-ups never want to believe in things like buried treasure. Even Mr Green doesn't believe in it. No — we would have to have real proof before we could go to Sergeant Dolan."

"But we have the proof," Essie insisted. "You could tell them you saw all those crucibles and things, and then they'd come and search the Big House."

Mike considered this for a minute and then shook his head. "No use, Essie. Even if they believed us — though I don't think they would — McFadden and Tobin would have the things well hidden by now. Don't forget they'll be on their guard ever since they caught Con and myself watching the other evening."

"What will you do then?"

The boys were silent as they turned the problem over in their minds. "There's only one thing to do," Con said slowly. "We'll have to find some way of getting into that house and finding out if McFadden really has found the treasure. If he has, we'll have to get real proof for the police. We'll have to take away a goblet or something to show them."

Essie's eyes grew round. "Oh, Con! wouldn't that be terribly dangerous? Supposing McFadden and Tobin caught you? They'd kill the two of you."

"We'll have to risk being caught," Con said. "What we can't risk is letting that pair melt down the treasure and clear out with it."

"We'd need to be quick about it, then," said Mike. "I've an idea that if we don't hurry we'll be too late."

"We'll have to get into the house while McFadden is out with the dog," Con decided. "Then we'd only have Tobin to escape from if we were caught. We'd have no chance at all against two men and a dog."

Essie was troubled. It made her heart thump to think of the two boys being cornered in that terrifying house. No treasure was worth such a risk, she felt. "I wish you'd forget about the old treasure," she said worriedly. "If mother knew what you're thinking of doing, she'd be mad with you, Con. And Big Bill would be mad with you, Mike."

Instantly, both boys looked at her sternly.

"Essie Byrne," Con said warningly, "if you tell —!"

"You promised you wouldn't, Essie," Mike reminded her.

CHAPTER NINE

MIKE and Con did not find it so easy to carry out their plan, after all. Each evening when supper was over, they lay in the heather and watched the Big House in the hope that Tobin would be left alone. Con watched the back of the house and Mike the front. But McFadden seemed to be taking no chances. The vicious dog remained constantly on guard, and his dour gaunt master seemed to have given up his lonely walks across the bog. Night after night, the boys watched and waited until darkness fell but the chance they hoped for did not come.

On the fourth evening they tried approaching the house cautiously from the back, but the wind was not in their favour and the dog scented them. He started to bark furiously, and they had no option but to take to their heels and get away before McFadden or Tobin should come out and discover them.

"It's easy enough for the fellows in story books," Mike grumbled as they trudged home. "They always have a piece of meat sprinkled with sleeping powder to throw to the watchdog. I wish we could get some sleeping powder for that brute."

The next day the drawing out of the turf was finished by dinner-time.

"Big Bill and myself will finish the clamping of it," Jem Byrne said. "You and Mike can take the ass and go into Clonboyle for a message for me. I want nails and screws and glue. Mr Rogan said he'd have them in this week. And I want you to collect the saw he sent up to Dublin to be fixed for me — he'll surely have it back by now. I'm lost without it." He made out a list of the things he wanted, and Con put it safely away in his pocket.

In Clonboyle they were jogging down the Main Street when Mike suddenly gripped his friend's arm. "Con! Con! Look who's standing beyond at Fleming's door."

Con looked across the street. It was McFadden. He was talking to Pat Fleming, the proprietor of Clonboyle's garage.

"Well, can you beat that?" Con exclaimed. "The old rogue goes and leaves Tobin by himself on the one day we're not there to grab our chance. What's he talking to Mr Fleming about, I wonder."

"Pull into the laneway here and we'll watch him," Mike said. Neddeen was driven into the laneway, and the boys jumped down. Keeping well out of sight, they watched McFadden. He seemed to be having an argument of some kind with Pat Fleming. Presently, the two men went into the garage together. After a little while, McFadden came out, mounted his rusty bicycle and rode off in the direction of his home.

"Wouldn't you give anything to know what he's up to?" Con said looking after him.

"I'm going to find out," said Mike quietly. "You stay here for a minute while I do a bit of detective work." He crossed the road to the garage.

The proprietor, to whom Mike and Big Bill were well

known, greeted him kindly. "What's troubling you, Mike? Are you coming to order a new Rolls Royce?"

Mike reddened. He felt ashamed of the trick he had to play on the man. "No, Mr Fleming. I — I was just wondering if you'd have a car going out our way this evening."

"Is it a lift home you're looking for? Not this evening, Mike. We won't have a car going your way till this day week. There's a man after leaving me — old McFadden, a neighbour of yours — and he ordered a car for this day week. He's off to Dublin, it seems. From all the questions he asked about the weight of stuff the car would carry, I'd say a lorry would be more in his line. He's a terrible man to strike a bargain, Mike, terrible hard. I was able for him, though — I got my price in the end. What's more, I got it in advance." Delighted to have someone to boast to of his triumph, Pat Fleming beamed at the boy. "Too bad I can't offer you a lift this evening, Mike. If you're in Clonboyle this day week you'll have one, and welcome."

"Thanks very much, Mr Fleming," Mike said gratefully. Pat Fleming went back into his office. He never guessed that it wasn't so much for the offer of a lift he had been thanked, as for some very useful information.

Mike ran back to where Con was waiting. "McFadden's clearing out," he said as he climbed into the cart. "He's going this day week. Drive on and I'll tell you."

"We'll *have* to make a move now!" was Con's comment when he heard the news. "Only a bare week left, Mike. What should we do?"

All the way home they thought and talked and argued. A hundred plans were suggested and cast aside. They had passed the Big House before they hit on a plan which seemed to offer some hope of success. They decided that one of them would climb on the front gate and attract the attention of the dog. The dog would give the alarm and bring out one of the men. Then, while man and dog were giving chase, the other boy would do his best to get into the house. If he succeeded, he would lie low in one of the rooms until McFadden and Tobin were asleep. As Con said, the two had to sleep *sometime*. They agreed to draw lots so as to decide which part each should play.

"I don't like it," Mike said. "It's very risky. And I'd rather the two of us would be together. Besides, it's ten to one against the door being left unguarded while the chase is going on. Still, we can chance it. When will we do it?"

"What about tomorrow night? We'll watch awhile to see would McFadden go out with the dog. If he doesn't we'll try out our plan." Happy with the decision they set off home.

They had not gone far when, above the creaking of the cart and the rattle of the ass's hooves, they heard their names called.

Mike looked back. "It's Essie, Con! Pull up." Essie was running to them over the marshy land at the left of the road. She was shouting something as she ran, and pointing back towards the new field where the cow had been put to graze.

Con pulled the ass in towards the side of the road. The two boys jumped down.

"What is it, Essie? What's wrong?" they called as they ran to meet her.

She was so breathless that at first they could hardly make out what she was saying.

"The calf!" Essie gasped. "Oh, come quick and get her out."

"Out from where, Essie?" Con demanded.

Essie gulped. "She fell down in a hole and a lump of the field fell in with her. She's not killed, but I couldn't get her out. I tried, but I couldn't lift her." By now the tears were streaming down poor Essie's face.

Mike was off in the direction of the field. "Come on, Con," he called over his shoulder. "Stop crying, Essie. We'll get her out all right for you."

The three children ran so quickly through the long grass that the tough stems of hard-heads and ryegrass lashed their legs like whips.

"This way!" Essie cried, running towards where a clump of gorse made a gold patch in the corner of the field. The patch was scarred by a yawning hole. The cow was standing beside the scene of the accident, lowing piteously, and bending her head now and then to peer down at where her calf was imprisoned.

Con and Mike jumped down into the hole which was about four feet deep. In spite of the earth which had fallen into it, there was room in it for themselves and the calf.

They ran their hands quickly over the frightened little creature.

"She's all right, Essie," Mike said. "No bones broken. We'll have her out of this for you in two ticks."

The boys got their shoulders under the calf and, grunting and straining, they heaved her up out of the hole and on to the field. For a second, she lay panting on her side while her mother nuzzled her. Then, to prove she had not been hurt, she struggled on to her spindly legs.

Essie put her arms around the calf's neck and hugged her fervently. It would have been hard to know whether she or the calf's mother was the happier.

"It was lucky the two of you came along just then," she kept saying. "I'll never forget it to you — never!"

Con clambered out of the hole. "What happened, anyway, Essie? How did the calf fall in? Didn't she see the hole, or what?"

"She couldn't have," Essie said, "because it wasn't there."

"How do you mean: it wasn't there?"

"Well —" Essie wrinkled her forehead as she tried to explain exactly how the accident had happened. "When I came for them, the cow was grazing over here beside this clump of gorse, and the calf beside her. Right where the big hole is now, I noticed a weeshie little hole, like a rabbit burrow. When I started to drive them home, the calf caught her foot in the little hole, and in she went and a lump of the field with her. Then it wasn't a little hole at all, but a great big one."

"It was a fox's hole," Con said. "Or maybe a badger's. It's a good thing the calf wasn't killed."

"I'd better be going. Mother will be wondering what's keeping me. Thanks again, lads." Essie started off across the field, driving the cow and calf before her.

"Are you coming, Mike?" Con was anxious to get home to his supper. "Or are you thinking of staying in the hole all night?"

"Come here a minute, Con. Come down here beside me. I want to show you something."

Con hesitated. He badly wanted his dinner, but there was something in Mike's tone that decided him. "Oh, all right then. But hurry up. I'm hungry." He called after Essie who was half-way across the field by now. "Tell mother we'll be home soon, Essie." He jumped into the hole beside his friend.

"Look, Con." Mike's voice was unsteady with excitement. "Did you ever hear of a badger or a fox building walls like these? Were the stones in these walls put there by men or by foxes?"

Con looked and gave a long low whistle. In front and behind, there was nothing but the heaped earth and furze bushes dislodged by the calf in her fall. But on each side of the hole, the walls were straight and even. They were built of hewn blocks of granite, fitted together as only a master mason could have fitted them. "You're right, Mike," he said. "This is no fox's den. What would it be, then? An old well?"

Mike shook his head. "I don't think so. It's more like a mineshaft, though I don't think it's that, either, for I never heard tell of mines in these parts. I think it's — I'm nearly afraid to say what I think it is."

"Go on Mike. Speak up." By now, Con was every bit as excited as Mike.

Mike was silent for a second. Then he said slowly, "You'll say I'm stupid, Con. But while Essie and you were talking, I had an idea. Come here and stand in front of me." Con did so. "Now look in a straight line where I'm pointing. What do you see?"

Con squinted along the line made by Mike's arm. "I see the rath at the back of the Big House. What about it?"

"Just this. I think the calf is after showing us a way into the Big House. I think that this hole isn't a mineshaft, or a well, or a badger's den. I think it's the entrance to a secret passage into the rath."

Con's eyes opened wide. "But how — why — who —?" he stuttered.

"Listen," Mike gripped his friend's arm. "It's well known that the fighting men of long ago had secret ways of getting in and out of their forts? Wouldn't Fionn have had one, too? He the wisest leader of them all!"

Even still, Con could not believe. "But wouldn't someone around the place have known about it? I never heard of such a passage and I never heard Granda talking about one either."

"He wouldn't have known. We wouldn't have known if it wasn't for the calf. The last man who used the passage — and Heaven only knows how long ago that was! — must have roofed it over with sods. Then gorse grew on all the sods, and not one ever guessed the passage was there. Lately, the roof must have started to crumble away — the little hole that Essie took for a rabbit-burrow was the beginning of it — and the calf's fall did the rest."

"It would be great if it were true," Con said. "But I'm afraid of my life, Mike, that you're dreaming, like when you're making up your poems."

"It'll be easy enough to find out whether I am or not," Mike retorted. "What's to prevent us bringing a couple of spades up here when the supper is over and shovelling away all the earth here in the front of the hole? We'd soon find out if I'm dreaming."

Mike seemed to have such faith in his idea that Con began to believe in it too. "Good!" he said. "I'm on. We'll come back the minute the supper is over." Then his face fell, and he groaned. "I forgot!" he said dolefully. "Mother is making me go to bed after the supper. Think of it! Bed! When I might be out on an adventure like this. We'd better hurry or there will be no supper left for us. Come on, Mike."

"Try to persuade your mother to let you out," Mike urged,

as they ran to where Neddeen patiently awaited them. "If we have to wait till tomorrow somebody else might discover the passage — maybe McFadden himself — and then everything would be spoiled."

The others had nearly finished their supper when the boys came in.

CHAPTER TEN

AFTER supper, Con and Mike sat fidgeting in their chairs, wondering if they dared ask to go out. In his big chair in the corner, Granda sat puffing his pipe and watching them through the clouds of smoke. The twinkle in his eye was brighter than ever. After a little while he took the pipe from his mouth.

"About that hole in the new field, Jem," he said with an innocent air. "Shouldn't it be railed in for fear the calf would fall in again? She mightn't get off so lucky the next time."

Jem Byrne groaned and put down his paper. "You're right I suppose. Oh, dear! and I thought I was going to have a nice quiet read and a smoke this evening. Ah well!"

He made to rise from his chair, but Granda put out his hand. "Can't the two young lads here do it for you? What do you say, lads? Would you have any objections?"

The boys had jumped to their feet. Hopefully, they looked at Mrs Byrne.

She considered it. "Would they ever be able to make the fence?"

"Of course we could do it, Mother," Con said eagerly.

"All right, then," Mrs Byrne agreed. "I meant you to go to bed early tonight, but seeing that your father is so tired you'd better go."

When they had collected the spades they needed, Mike went on up the road while Con went back to the house for the hammer.

Essie met him at the door with it. "I'm coming too, Con," she told him. "Mother said I could."

For a minute Con thought everything was going to be upset, but then he realised that Essie might be very useful. She could keep watch. "Come on, then," he said. "I've something to tell you when we get out on the road." They joined Mike, and Essie was told what they proposed to do.

Back in the kitchen, Granda got to his feet and hobbled to the gate. He looked out at the children. "Spades," he said to himself. "Now what do they want the spades for? There's something going on here and it must be something dangerous or they'd have told me about it." He watched them until his tired old eyes could no longer see them, and all the time his worry grew.

After a while he made up his mind. "I'm going to take a walk up the road, Mary," he called. "I'll go as far as the new field and I'll be back with the children." Leaning heavily on his stick, he started up the road.

It did not take them long to make the fence. Con drove in the stakes while Essie held them for him, and then they ran the rope around the barricade. Meanwhile, Mike cut branches of thorn with which he strengthened the fence. This done, the boys started on the real work of the evening. They jumped down into the hole and started to shovel feverishly. Their arms were aching and they were feeling they must have moved a ton of earth when Mike gave a shout of triumph.

"Hurrah, Con! I was right!"

Their spades had uncovered a low arch built of the same

110

regular slabs of granite which formed the walls. The archway was choked with earth, but soon they had it cleared and a dark passage yawned in front of them.

Con looked at Mike. "I take back all I said," he said generously. "You have a great head for thinking things out, Mike," and pushing him aside he proceeded to enter the archway, torch in hand. But Mike pulled him back.

"Oh, no you don't, Con. The idea about the passage was mine. If there's any danger in it, I should be the one to go first."

"We'll draw for it," Con said. "Hold two blades of grass, Essie. Whichever of us draws the long one will go first."

"Mike Fahy! Con Byrne!" Essie was horrified at the thought of them going into that dark, evil-smelling passage. "You must be out of your minds to think of going in there."

"Don't be silly, Essie," Con said. "What do you think we're after breaking our backs shovelling for? Just to stand and look at the passage?"

"It's our only chance of getting into the Big House, Essie," Mike told her. "Con and myself had another plan but it would never have worked out. This is our only chance to catch out McFadden. We'll be all right. Con has his torch."

There was nothing Essie could do but hold the blades of grass for them. Mike drew the longer one. With Con's torch in his left hand, he stooped under the low archway. Once inside, he found he could stand upright.

"Keep a sharp look-out," Con warned his sister. "It isn't likely that anyone would come this way, and even if they do, the fence makes a good screen. But if you see McFadden or Tobin coming, stoop down into the tunnel and give three good blows with the hammer on the stone. That will give us warning. And then you make for home as fast as you can."

"All right," Essie faltered. "I'll — I'll keep guard for you."

The passage ran straight before them as far as the torch-beam could reach. It was a dank place, and the air was foul and heavy. Slime trickled from the roof and oozed from the walls. Sickening grey-white creatures like bats flitted about their heads and blundered into their faces. Monstrous rats scuttled along beside them, brushing against their legs and gazing up at them with little evil eyes. And under their feet the boys felt horrible squelching things. It was a nightmare journey. They had been creeping along for what seemed like hours but what was in reality no more than fifteen minutes when a slab of rock loomed up in front of them. It blocked the passage. They could go no further.

Con and Mike looked at each other in dismay.

"That's fixed it!" Con exclaimed. "What are we going to do now?"

"We must be up against the rath," Mike warned. "Maybe McFadden and Tobin are on the other side of that rock. We don't want them to hear us."

Con eyed the rock that barred their way. "Maybe it doesn't go right up to the roof," he said. "Maybe there would be enough space at the top to let us squeeze through. I'm going to climb up and have a look."

This was more easily said than done. The smooth face of the rock was slithery with slime. Again and again he tried but he could get no foothold.

"Couldn't you stand on my shoulder?" Mike suggested. "There's a little bit of rock jutting out there up near the top. If you stood on my shoulder you could get a grip on it and then maybe you could pull yourself up."

112

He stooped down. Con climbed onto his friend's shoulder. Slowly he raised himself and stretched his arms until his fingers found the little ledge. He felt Mike's shoulders trembling under the strain of supporting him. "Just a minute more, Mike," he whispered. "Hold on till I get a good grip."

At that very moment a rat leaped blindly. He struck against Mike's face. At the feel of the loathsome hairy body Mike staggered backwards — he could not help it. He fell, dropping the torch, and Con was left dangling with his full weight on the bit of rock. He felt it shift in his hands. Slowly it shifted. The next minute the slab of rock was moving outwards, very, very stiffly like a door that has not opened for centuries. It opened about a foot, and then stopped. Con dropped to the ground and Mike scrambled to his feet. They squeezed through the opening. For a second, they were too dazed to take in anything. Then they saw they were in a small round cave.

"We're under the rath!" Mike whispered.

The place was like a rabbit-warren with tunnels. At every yard a tunnel had been made. Some of them were only half-begun. Others of them extended far into the earth. Over the entrance to the largest of them hung a smoky lantern.

As they looked around, the boys saw that from this side the door through which they had entered looked like nothing but a huge rock. The secret passage had been well hidden.

"It's good to know we have a quick way out in case we have to make a run for it," Con said.

"Listen!" Mike held up a finger. "Isn't that McFadden's voice?"

They listened. Though they could not make out what was being said, they heard the voices of McFadden and Tobin.

The murmur came from the direction of the biggest of the tunnels. The boys crept to the entrance and looked down. It was about twenty yards long, and seemed to lead into another cave. From where they stood they could see a great uneven heap of something that winked and glittered with a pale, yellow gleam.

"The treasure!" Mike breathed. Con did not answer. He could only stare goggle-eyed at that heap of gold. As if drawn by a magnet, they tip-toed further down the tunnel. Now they could see the treasure clearly, the goblets studded with blood-red rubies, the great heavy dishes, the rings and bracelets in which diamonds winked, and the girdles and collars, yellow and bright. Now, too, they could hear the men's words distinctly.

Alert, and ready to run at the first hint of discovery, the boys crouched in the tunnel and listened.

"You're a twister!" Tobin was saying, and his voice was thick with anger. "Cheat! Twister! Rogue! Set me free and give me my share of the treasure!"

"What a fool you are, Tobin," McFadden was almost purring. "When you drank the whiskey I brought you from Clonboyle you never suspected there was a sleeping draught in it. The surprised look on your stupid face as you dropped off to sleep almost made me laugh. It was really funny, Tobin, but not nearly so funny as your expression when you woke up and found yourself tied hand and foot." The man laughed and the sound of that laugh sent a feeling of cold horror over the listening boys.

"And is this what I'm after slaving these twenty years for?" Tobin demanded with helpless fury. "Is this what I get after living for twenty years in this prison of a place?"

114

"You're forgetting something, Tobin." McFadden continued to speak with shaky softness. "This prison, as you call it, has not been nearly so bad as the real prison from which you had escaped that night over twenty years ago when you came to me and begged me to hide you."

"You were glad enough to see me that night!"

"Oh, yes. I admit I saw at once you would be useful. But for your help, I might have found it difficult to break open that old fool's safe and take the money and the manuscript. I admit too that you have been very useful in digging the tunnels and in various other ways. But now you're of no further use to me, Tobin. I have the treasure now, and it's mine — all mine.

"Twister! Rogue!" howled Tobin. "Give me my share!"

McFadden went on without heeding him. It was almost as if he were speaking to himself. "The treasure is mine. I earned it. It was my brain that decoded the manuscript — my genius that planned everything. My wisdom that foresaw all danger and planned against it — just as I foresaw that you might try to get away with the gold. Fool! Did you think I would risk having you rob me at the last moment?"

"Twenty years of slavery!" Tobin said bitterly. "Twenty years of slavery!"

"*You* speak of slavery!" A different note crept into McFadden's voice now. "It's only for slavery that stupid fools like you are fitted. What of me, a man of genius? What of the twenty precious years I have spent in finding this treasure? What of the long years I spent working on the manuscript until at last I had the magic words: *In the cave beyond the rath the treasure of Fionn lies waiting*. And what of the years of disappointment that came later when one tunnel after

116

another was made, each of them in turn leading nowhere? If the treasure were twice what it is it would not be enough to pay me. Bah! Why should I waste my time talking to you? There is still work to be done — the remainder of the gold to be carried to the laboratory. This must be done tonight, Tobin, so that tomorrow I may start to melt it down. And when I have carried the last of the gold from this cave I will close up the mouth of the tunnel and leave you here for a long, long sleep—"

"No, no!" The man's voice was wild with terror. "You wouldn't do that! You're bad, but you wouldn't do that!"

"Wouldn't I, Tobin? We'll see. It's for your own good, my friend. Shut away here in this quiet place you will be spared the pain of having to look on while I melt down my beautiful gold. You won't even hear the car that will come to take me and my gold away. Am I not thoughtful, Tobin, to consider your feelings?"

He laughed again, but Tobin's voice broke in on the laugh. "Go on; laugh! You won't laugh long. You are the fool! Wait

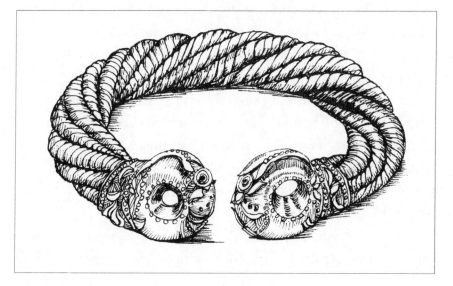

till they start asking questions around here. The driver of the car will be able to put them on your track. Then you'll laugh! You'll laugh when you're dangling at the end of a rope. If only I could be there to see it!"

"No one will ever see that, Tobin," McFadden answered with dreadful quietness. "The driver of the car will not put them on my track. He will never tell where he drove me. When I have finished with him next week, he will be as silent as you will be by then, my friend."

There was a sound of grunting and heavy breathing, and the listening boys guessed that Tobin was straining at his bonds.

"Don't tire yourself, Tobin," they heard McFadden say. "You won't get those bonds off — I tied them tightly."

At that moment, the boys heard another sound which took their attention from the two rogues. It was a slow tap-tap-tap. It came from behind them. Tap-tap-tap! Tap-tap-tap! Though faint and indistinct, they recognised it. They had heard it too often to be mistaken. It was the sound of Granda's stick and it was coming nearer and nearer. They looked at each other in dismay. Surely Granda was not coming along the secret passage? If he was, he must be stopped — turned back — warned of the danger towards which he was limping.

Con opened his mouth to yell, but the warning shout never came, for McFadden's arm was about his neck, almost strangling him. His other arm was around Mike in a similar stranglehold. Their struggling was useless against that grip of iron, and they found themselves dragged back into the treasure cave.

McFadden was blind and deaf with fury. Keeping his hold on the boys, he dragged them to where Tobin lay struggling

118

against his bonds.

"You fool!" he screamed at the man. "This is more of your stupidity! I trusted you to keep the windows and doors locked, and look at the result!"

In spite of their terror and pain, a quick surge of thankfulness rose in the boys. McFadden knew nothing of the secret passage! Maybe Granda could be saved yet. If only he could be kept from hearing the tap-tap-tap of the stick. They kicked and scuffled their feet on the floor, but McFadden's grip tightened around their necks until they felt their lungs bursting for want of air and their legs go limp.

Frantically, Tobin was trying to free himself. He rolled and twisted and worked himself in this direction and that. His struggles carried him over the floor until he was wedged between the wall and a huge bronze chest. The din made by his heavy boots against the bronze was ear-splitting, but McFadden's screams were louder still.

"Now you'll have company, Tobin!" he shouted. "These two will stay with you when I leave you tonight. They will die as all who get in my way must die!" Savagely, he shook the boys and his murderous grip around their necks became ever tighter. The blood drummed loudly in their ears, their eyes were bursting from the sockets and they felt themselves growing faint. A darkness was falling on them when the grip suddenly became slack. It loosened, and McFadden's arms dropped from around their necks. The next instant the man lay in a crumpled heap on the floor.

They staggered and blinked while their lungs gulped air. Gradually, the drumming in their ears ceased and their sights cleared. It was only then that they saw Granda standing beside them. His eyes were twinkling, and he was looking in a surprised, innocent way at the sledge-hammer in his hand. "I gave him just the tiniest little tap with it," he was saying. "Just the softest, tiniest little tap on the back of the head. And look at the sweet sound sleep he's in."

McFadden stirred and groaned.

"He's not sleeping so sound after all," said Granda. "Just in case he'd wake up lads, can one of you sit on his chest and the other sit on his legs."

Half-dazed the boys obeyed.

"Hey!" Tobin shouted from his corner. "Come over here and open these cords."

Granda looked at him. "I think you'll be all right as you are till the police get here," he said. "Keep yourself quiet now, or maybe you'd have to be put to sleep like your master here." He brandished the sledge-hammer threateningly, and Tobin huddled back without a word.

"But — how did you get here, Granda?" Con asked when he had recovered his breath.

"And in the darkness of the tunnel!" Mike marvelled.

"What darkness are you talking about?" said Granda. "You left the torch lying on the ground all nice and handy to light the way for me."

"But how did you know we were here?" Con wanted to know.

"That's simple," replied Granda. "I was having a little walk when I came upon Essie and she sitting in that hole. The poor child was nearly dead wondering what was happening to the two of you. I said I'd follow you and find out, and I sent her home for your father and Big Bill, just in case they'd be needed. I brought along the hammer for fear of trouble — and very useful it was too." The old man's voice took on a huffy note. "But I'm not too pleased with the two of you for trying to keep me out of this adventure."

"Well, it was this way, Granda," Mike began, a little shamefacedly. "We thought —"

"You thought that just because I'm an old man I'd be a spoil-sport. You should have known. Well, maybe I'll forgive you for this time — but only on condition that you start at the beginning and tell me every word of it while we're waiting for the others."

Between them they told him the whole story.

"And there's the treasure," Con concluded, pointing to the heap of gold. "Some of it, at least. From what we heard McFadden say, there must be a lot more of it out in the cellar, all ready to be melted down."

Granda limped over to the glittering heap. He looked at it thoughtfully. "So that's the stuff that men are willing to rob and kill and fight for? Well, Well! I'd rather be looking at a field of ripe wheat any day in the week."

"McFadden is waking, Granda," Mike said in a sudden alarm. "Will we ever be able to hold him down?"

"Don't worry," Granda answered. "If he shows any fight, the hammer will soon quieten him again."

But Granda didn't have to use the hammer after all, for just then Jem Byrne and Big Bill arrived, and shortly after them came Sergeant Dolan and his men.

CHAPTER ELEVEN

IT was a month later. Through the warm August evening, laughter and happy voices were mingled with the music that drifted over the bog. They were having a party in the cottage to celebrate the generous reward the boys had received for preventing the loss of Fionn's treasure, now safe in the National Museum.

They were all there. Even Aunt Sarah had come down from Dublin. Mr Green, too. Mike had insisted that the party could not be held without him. "Only for Mr Green's book," he said, "McFadden would have got away with the gold."

The kitchen was a happier place than ever that evening of the party, with Mrs Byrne handing around plates of good things, and everyone talking and eating and laughing.

Suddenly Granda called for silence.

"I want to propose another toast," he said, lifting his cup. "We already had a toast to Mr Green for setting the lads on the track of the treasure. We drank to Aunt Sarah who was the means of them getting to know Mr Green, and to Uncle Pat and Dinny for taking them to Dublin. There was even a toast to the Mammy here for letting them go, and even to the *Maggie May* that carried them — and well they deserved it, and to Jem and Big Bill for coming to the rescue. There was a toast to myself for the little part I played. But there's one toast we didn't drink yet." Granda looked into his cup for a minute before he went on. "A few months back," he said slowly, "there was talk in this house of selling the calf. Everyone was for it, except Essie here. Essie had a great love for that calf. She begged and begged for it to be let stay. She offered to take full care of it herself. She said she'd give up her play morning and evening to look after it. She said she'd do anything on earth if only it would not be sold. Well, thanks to Essie, the calf was let stay. You all know what happened. Only for the calf the secret passage would never have been found. The boys would never have got into that house, and McFadden and his friend wouldn't be safe in jail now, and the gold would not be safe in the Museum. Mike and Con wouldn't be going away to college next month, nor would the rest of us be sitting here snug and comfortable, knowing that there's plenty in the bank to keep us all from worry for as long as we live. Here's my toast to you, then: To Essie and the calf."

"To Essie and the calf!" they all answered and drained their cups.

THE END